CHASING EXTINCTION

The Chasing Series: Book Three

RM HAMRICK

Cover design by Covers by Christian
Editing by Sticks and Stones Editing

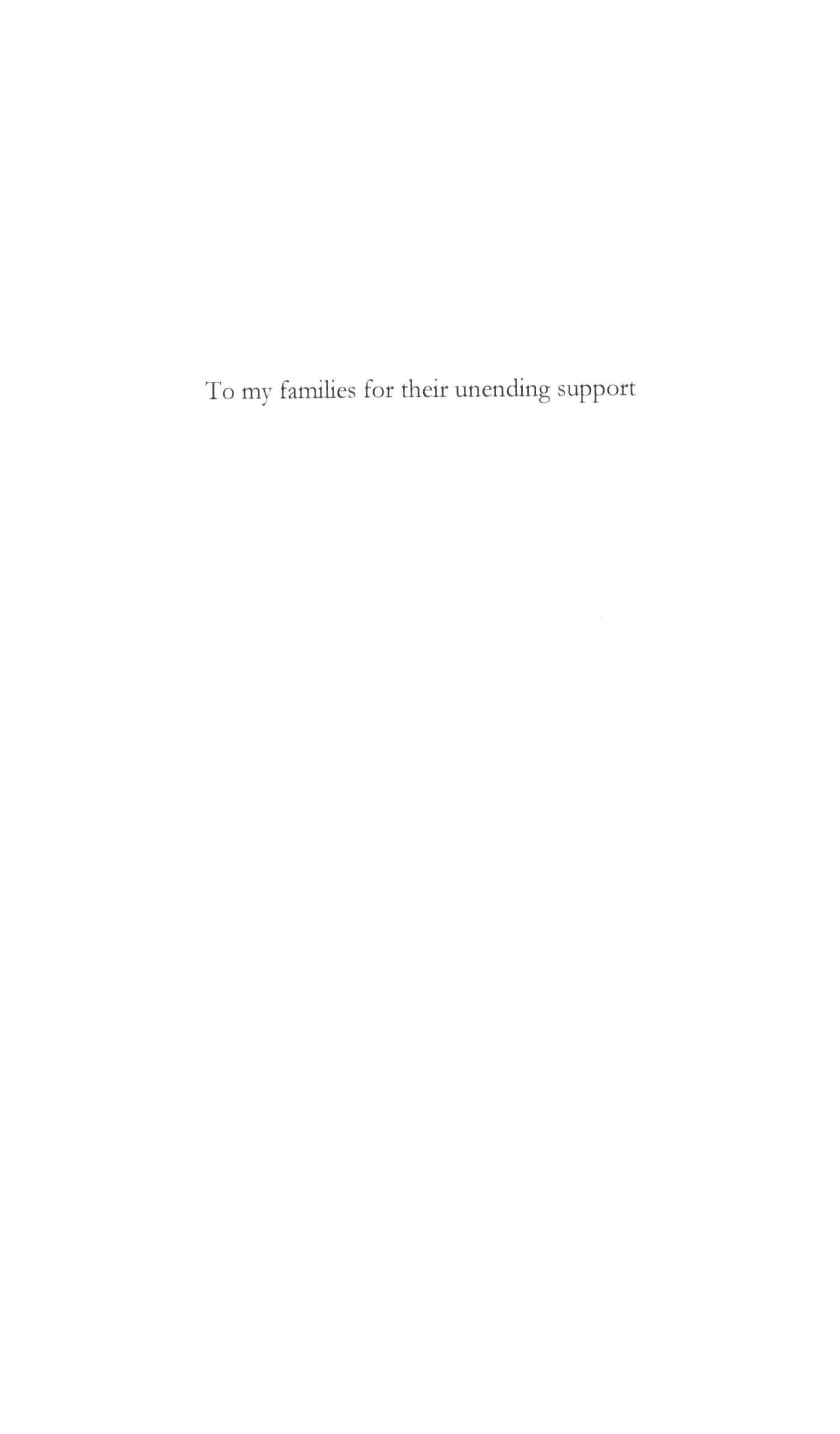

To my families for their unending support

CHAPTER ONE
COURIER

The oak leaf litter, muddled browns and rich blacks, muffled Audra's footsteps. But the bare trees did little to shield her approach as her short, lithe frame climbed through the Georgian brush. Pearl skin and speckled green eyes flashed underneath a thin hood which she adjusted over her hair. Although summer's coppery highlights were fading back to their chocolaty auburn, it remained in sharp contrast to the colors of a bleak winter.

Audra felt the outline of the scrawled letter through her threadbare jacket. She'd have to remember to put it in her pack if it rained. She hadn't delivered mail in a long while. Not since a simpler time. But, it allowed her to do the one thing she could do.

Run.

Darting through the forest was Audra's specialty and priceless in this world where escaping a zombie's bite meant you lived another day. Audra's life had centered around running. First, running for Lysent Corporation as she tried to secure a cure for her bitten sister. Then, she ran for Osprey Point to secure a cure for everyone.

Both failures on her account.

No one in her group could make sense of the formerly cured people turning back into shambling shells. Their treatment for the z-virus did not seem permanent. While Larange Greenly of Lysent blamed it on Osprey Point's 'reckless incompetence', Jack from Washington DC reported Lysent's antiviral was just as temporary.

Gordon had just located his family, but now with the risk of reversion hanging heavy, he refused to reunite with them. Instead, Audra carried his letter — a notification he was currently alive and thought of them often, and also a goodbye.

Audra wasn't sure why she should be running anymore. It was all for naught, just lies she had believed. Just lies she had told herself.

Audra's stomach grumbled.

Winter wasn't a lie.

She surveyed the ground for something to settle the churning in her gut. Tracks of a nearby animal to hunt was asking for too much. She'd dig up some acorns buried by squirrels or dandelion roots sleeping through the winter — anything to make her salivate and lie to her stomach that food was on the way.

She should have packed rations for her journey, but splitting their stores between Osprey Point and their new quarantine location had made it startlingly clear there was not enough food for either group's winter. As they divvied up their fall harvest of hickory nuts, chicory roots, and the like, it was clear winter foraging would be a daily task.

She couldn't take from their supplies.

But, she had also forgotten the difficulties of blazing a trail. This wasn't walking through her well-worn paths around Osprey Point or Lysent rail lines. This was navigating to a town far from the Lysent network with no clear route. Audra had forgotten how much energy it took to keep in the right direction and hike through the brush. Maybe she'd risk taking the roads back. But unfamiliar roads meant unfamiliar people and possible traps. Easy moving might turn into easy dying.

Audra moved from maple tree to maple tree, pulling the shriveled winged seeds from branches, shaking off the cobwebs. Flavors would differ from tree to tree, but winter declared they would all be bitter. Still, snapping the wing off and popping the seed pod into her mouth — it was better than nothing.

Audra recalled Gordon's directions to find the town. It had to be close. Maybe not close enough. Or maybe she was lost. The sky's grey whiteness vaguely lit the forest, but also hid the time from her. She pushed forward. The cool day would lead to a cold night she wouldn't want to suffer in her flimsy summer tent. She needed walls. Shelter.

While she was sure the letter would find its way in, she wasn't so sure if she'd be allowed to accompany it. Audra and Osprey Point no longer had anything of value to offer. She'd cross that bridge when she came to it. For now, she just wanted to find the small town before the sun tumbled from its hidden perch.

*   *   *

Audra all but stumbled upon her destination. She had been sure she was lost, but the small main street with its defunct traffic light popped up in the wood. A few shops barely justified it being called a town before. Now, it was tired and ghostly. It would be like any other small hub for farming neighbors, except for the giant chain grocery store just on the outskirts which had seen its demise before the world's end. Audra imagined that the store had gone out of business just as quickly as it had popped up, leaving a parking lot that would never be filled and a building much too large for anyone to utilize. Until now.

The curb against the road had been stacked with overturned grocery carts, creating a barrier of materialistic waste from the droves. Every defense against the zoms risked drawing the attention of marauders. This wall of coated metal carts was a shiny beacon for those looking to take. Audra refused to underestimate them and took caution as she scooted through the opening in the carts.

A few feet onto the concrete parking lot were parked cars, lined bumper to bumper. The path to the green sedan in the center looked well-traveled. Audra found the driver's door to be unlocked and most of the interior gutted. Audra slid through to the other side, where she opened the passenger door and slipped out. There, another line-up of cars, this time an opening between two of them. She looked over the row to find more vehicles, all positioned purposefully.

Settled dust on hoods and roofs indicated the residents carefully walked around them for their ingress and egress. Maybe to shed doubt on the store's occupancy, or perhaps to keep scent trails intact. It was a maze or a queue, really — a way to slow small groups of wanderers. It wouldn't stop a large herd though. They'd just flood over the cars.

Audra pulled a rag out of her bag. It wasn't white but it would have to do. She didn't want to be mistaken for the sick. Holding it over her head, she walked the circuitous path.

When in Rome.

As she finally reached the store front on the other end of the parking lot, she heard a throat clear above her. She looked up to see a long rifle pointed at her from the roof, steadied on a rusty security camera. 50/50 the rifle was loaded. 20/80 he could shoot and wasn't just up there for show. Behind the rifle was a ruddy face with a bulbous nose.

Audra waved her little raggedy flag once more.

"I'm Audra. I've got mail for someone inside."

"Mail?" the man pulled his face away from the rifle, and used a hand to scratch the back of his head in thought.

"Yeah, for Haleigh and Eliza Bottman," she said as if postal work was common. "Do you have anyone here by those names?"

His round shoulders shrugged. "Do you have any weapons on you?"

"Just my blades."

He nodded his head towards the entrance.

Her word was enough?

Guess he didn't think much of her. Audra had assumed defenses would be tight, considering their flashy entrance. Instead, Audra couldn't find reason this place was unmolested. Seemed they let anyone in.

Either side of the windowed front wall had been reinforced with freezer units filled with cash registers and other worthless machines. Audra walked through the entrance. On either side lay the previously sliding doors and boxes to support them for closing up for the night.

A woman with short curly hair streaked with silver, and deep lines in her bronzed face approached Audra and without introduction, she brusquely patted her down. Her hands ran down Audra's body. They paused at the knives, feeling size and features. Guess they wouldn't take her word for it after all.

"Where ya from?" she asked, folding her arms over an oversized army fatigue jacket.

"Osprey Point. It's a —"

"We know Osprey Point."

"You do?" Audra was surprised.

"Is it true you have a cure?" she asked curtly. Her flinty demeanor cracked as her brows furrowed into one. She stared down at Audra with one hip cocked, waiting.

Audra found she couldn't voice the words. She shook her head. They had no cure. The woman didn't need to hear it out loud. Her face settled back into its grim features and stiff expression.

Now, bad news was just news, but still its delivery wasn't Audra's forte. She hadn't even fully entered the establishment, and she already wished to be done and gone — despite winter's nightly bite.

"Do you know where I can find Haleigh and Eliza Bottman?" Audra asked.

The woman gave the same nod as the man outside had. "Black woman and a little girl? They're in the produce section."

The answer confused her for a moment before she recovered and copied their nod. The dimness of winter came through the store's skylights, illuminating grocery store aisle signs. Faded in color, they hung from the ceiling, outlasting the time when shelves upon shelves were stocked with cardboard- and plastic-wrapped food.

Now those shelves had been arranged to create stalls for the living. Some of the families appeared to be in transit. Others, as if they'd been here for several years. Audra walked toward the back corner previously for produce. Some of the cubiclees had curtains. Others had not managed such privacy. But in each cubicle, the soft glow of lanterns unsuccessfully fought the bleary evening.

A group of children giggled, danced, and skipped past her, ignoring the gloom of the weather. Audra wasn't sure if Eliza was in the short-statured crowd, but they all appeared healthy and washed. The place did feel a bit like a sanctuary with its tall walls and ceilings, but Audra couldn't help but consider it was only protected by a wall of shopping carts, a few cars, and a man on the roof. What would stop a group from coming in and robbing or killing them?

In the produce section, the display coolers had all been removed, leaving dark scuffs and electrical outlets where they once stood. Audra tried her best to casually glance into stalls for a sign of Haleigh or her daughter. Toward the corner, she spotted a woman with dark hair pulled back by a kerchief. She was tall and slender. The woman, as if she felt eyes on her, turned. She wore long flowing slacks cinched tight around her waist, and a soft jersey tank underneath a moth-eaten sweater.

"Haleigh Bottman?" Audra asked.

Her brown doe eyes blinked as the skin around them wrinkled a bit.

"Yes?" She wrung the scrap of cloth she was using to dust.

Audra had spent most of her hike rehearsing ways

to tell this woman her 'long-dead' ex-husband had written them a note. None of her approaches seemed great. She'd go for simple.

"I'm Audra. I'm carrying a letter from Gordon for you."

"Ta— what?" she stuttered. Her arms came out in surprise, hitting the LED lantern.

Despite her ill-fitting clothes and some security vulnerabilities, Haleigh had a good setup here. And if Gordon's reconnaissance was correct, she also had a husband. It crossed Audra's mind that Haleigh might not want to read the letter.

In the swinging light, the woman found her way to her cot and sat down.

"Is he—?" she whispered.

Audra didn't know how to answer that. He hadn't written it years ago if that's what she meant.

"It's complicated. I'm sure his letter explains," she said as she reached for the letter from her coat.

Audra was surprised by her body's own frailness underneath the layers. Winter was making everything bare. No matter.

Haleigh's intentions for the letter were made clear as she snatched it from Audra's hands. Audra gave it freely.

Haleigh's eyes swept the handwriting before she clasped it to her chest. Large orb tears rolled down her cheek. She whimpered again before she pulled the letter back into her sights. Audra wondered if she could even read it with the glassy tears distorting her vision.

Audra felt a rare amount of social awkwardness as she waited for Haleigh. She looked from side to side of the aisle, but there really wasn't any place to go. She settled on sitting against the edge of their stall wall, her back toward Haleigh. Audra refused to see the fall of her face as she reached the letter's conclusion. Audra would never have written a letter like this. Why give them possibility just to rip it away again?

A tall, gangly girl whipped around the corner with a giant smile overtaking her face. Her hair flew behind her, the coils bouncing to a stop on her shoulders as she skidded to avoid Audra. The girl had some of Gordon's features, although Audra couldn't name them. Eliza's dark brown eyes darted from Audra to her mother and back to Audra again, flashing with accusation. Audra had done something to make her mother cry.

"Please, leave us alone," she whispered in passing.

Audra's eyes followed the girl as she wrapped her mother in her small arms. The gray cot sagged under their combined weight. Even though Eliza was only eight, Audra imagined she had a good sense of how to read and comfort her mother. Audra understood the dynamic well; emotional stability of your family dictated your survival. At eight years old, Eliza was an expert.

"I don't think I understand," Haleigh confessed. The wobble in her voice echoed in the cubicle.

Audra stood up, peeling out of her pack and leaving it on the cracked tiled floor. Back in their alcove, Eliza had weaseled herself between the letter and her mother, as if to protect her from it. Eliza stared down at the words, although Audra wasn't sure if she could read. Did they have schools in this place? From the giggles and shouts, it sounded as if they had enough children for it.

"Earlier this year I went with some scientists and

cleared out a laboratory, the one your husband worked at."

"Ex-husband. And 'lived at' would be more accurate." Her comment more matter-of-fact than bitter.

"Ex-husband," Audra corrected herself. "He'd been bitten. We treated him with a replicated antidote we stole from Lysent Corp. He was healthy again and was looking for you. But, it turns out the cure we gave him wasn't an enduring treatment. He's going to turn back into a zo— sick."

"Is there anything you can do for him?" Her chin rested on her daughter's head as she held her close.

"We're trying to figure out what went wrong so we can fix it… There's a lot of unknowns. It might take some time. It might be impossible."

She nodded, unsurprised. Outside of Lysent, many people hadn't heard more than rumors about a cure. And what sounded too good to be true, usually was.

With the crux of her mission complete, Audra needed to tend to other necessities. "I'm sorry, it's getting dark. Would it be OK if I slept on the floor of your… establishment… for the night?" she asked.

"Oh yes, of course." Haleigh rose immediately, letting her daughter fall to her feet. "And some food. Eliza, get the girl some food. Oh, I'm sorry — what's your name?"

"Audra."

"Thank you for doing this for us, Audra. You are kind to go out of your way in the winter to deliver a letter."

"Anything for Gordon. He's saved my life more than once. I wish there was more I could do."

In fact, Audra wished there was anything she could

do. When it came to beakers and protein markers, Audra was at a loss. She couldn't even figure out why Satomi always reprimanded her for calling it an 'antidote'.

Eliza offered Audra some brown fruit leather. After thanking her, she couldn't help but tear into it. She was so hungry. The sticky sweet stuck more to her teeth than landed in her stomach. Still, she was grateful. She worked pieces down with her tongue.

"Thank you," said Audra, feeling her lips stick to her jaw with each word. "I'll sleep here tonight. That will give you a chance to write your response, if you'd like. I'm sure he'd love to hear from you."

"It will give us a chance to pack," said Haleigh simply.

Audra raised her eyebrows. To pack?

"You will take us to see Gordon," Haleigh explained, riffling through a box of supplies.

Audra hadn't read the letter, but she was pretty sure that's not what it said. Gordon was clear. He didn't want Haleigh and Eliza to watch him turn into a zombie.

Next to the box sat a pack — large enough for a woman and a girl in times of transition. Audra wondered how many times they'd run. If they didn't start with additional guards on the perimeter, it might come again soon.

"Don't you have ties here?" reasoned Audra, noting at the same time how small the cot in the cubicle was. Was Gordon incorrect on the fact she was remarried?

"Kayle is dead," she said as if Audra had known his name. Her eyes seemed to recede, lost in grief's shadow. "Happened last week. On a run. I'll have to take his place."

Take his place on the run?

Haleigh's voice became distant and hollow. "I don't want to. What if something happens? What will happen to Eliza?"

Audra didn't have answers for Haleigh, except that her own volatile community wasn't the place for a young orphan. It wasn't really a place for anyone. Audra hadn't given much thought to how much more difficult life would be with a child.

There hadn't been many to remind her.

"I don't remember my dad," said Eliza, looking Audra in the eye, her mouth small. Audra could tell she was collecting information. Her mom's thought on death, for one.

"He remembers you, love. But he's sick. You can't go see him." The first half for Eliza and the second half to benefit her mother.

"We need to be there for him," said Haleigh. "No one should do this alone."

She mindlessly moved things around, waffling in her packing. Audra felt restless in the stale air. She had only brought trouble to this small family.

"We were alone," Eliza said, pulling on her mother's sleeve.

"He's not alone," assured Audra. "We have an entire quarantine area," she offered dumbly.

Haleigh ignored Audra's comment. Her long fingers danced in the girl's hair as she spoke to her. "We had each other. That is never alone. And your father needs someone too."

To hell with that. There was no way Audra was removing them from the produce section. Gordon's fate had haunted their dreams for years, but they'd never be able to discard the real sight of a cold decrepit shell and the shallow gray eyes. Audra's dreams were testaments to that.

Eliza's eyes were bright and sharp.

They would remain that way.

"I cannot take you," Audra said firmly. "Thank you for the food. I'll come by for your letter in the morning." Maybe hinting that she'd leave would settle the matter.

"No, please, stay," resigned Haleigh. Eliza's eyes slanted at the request, but she said nothing as her mother turned her to the small pail in the corner to wash up.

Audra appreciated the conversation's end. Her legs felt like they might collapse under her weight. She pulled from her feet the pieces of leather which once resembled shoes, before she slumped against a shelving wall. The air didn't feel quite as stale from her resting position. In fact, the warmth and humidity of a community enclosed in walls was almost comforting. Audra didn't have to worry about more pleas, she was fast asleep before they could fall on her ears.

CHAPTER TWO
COMPLICATIONS

Satomi lay on her hay-filled mattress as she finished counting the imagined rows of tiles on the ceiling of her dark room. She stared at them so often, she felt she could see them even when the sunlight faded and her lantern burned out. The edges glowed, burned into her sight. Maybe she could see them.

Her long black hair created a nest for her head on a pillow filled with folded worn clothes. She barely turned her heart-shaped face, fearing movement would chase away any sleep to be had. The window now in view, her almond-shaped eyes found nothing but soft moonlight filtering in.

Satomi surrendered to another night of sleeplessness by finally moving from her static pose. Her arm silently swept the blanket beside her.

No one.

Ryder had left for the quarantine location, leaving Satomi to work on the antiviral. Satomi didn't want to be apart from Ryder. More so, she didn't want Ryder in a place where its inhabitants could become driven to eat their roommates. The virus was dangerous again — not containable. And Ryder wasn't as scared as she should be.

Satomi felt Ryder's missing panic rising within herself. Her separation from her partner at least allowed her to sink into distress without an audience. A couple months had passed since she was penned in a police car like an animal, but still the fear and restlessness remained like a massive entity attached to her being. It left no room for others, isolating Satomi from friends. It loomed over her and threatened to expand so much that there'd be no room left for Satomi either.

Her skin crept and crawled underneath the blanket until she was convinced something was in the bed with her. Throwing off the blanket, she sat straight up. Sweat beaded along her hairline and fell in droplets off her legs. Breathing in the room's stagnant, musty air gave no relief.

She jumped out of bed, grabbed her jacket, and raced to the door. There, she came to an abrupt stop, willing herself to move with quiet composure. No need to wake anyone. Nothing was actually wrong, right?

That's not the way it felt.

She slipped into the hallway and followed the light of the lobby. The sounds of her feet were deadened by the rough nylon carpeting. The coolness of the tile floor preceded her escape out the door. There, cold air bit into her face. Outside, she heaved as if she'd been holding her breath for the moonlight and dew.

Maybe she had.

The ragged concrete felt cool on her feet. Weeds wrestled through the cracks and tickled whatever they could reach. Satomi walked from the sleeping quarters toward the center of the industrial park. The park's fence and laboratory had been invaluable at the start and the scattered one-story buildings had been re-purposed for their community. When Satomi had first arrived here with the other scientists, she was filled with hope. Now her hope had dried up like the cracked fountain sitting in the plaza.

Satomi sat on the ground against the fountain's walls. Her arms began to prickle, her jacket unworn beside her. Her olive skin had paled and yellowed with the winter, and the moonlight reflecting off the orange-hued limestone walls gave her an odd glow. She couldn't see the osprey statue in the center of the pool from her spot, but she imagined it diving down for its kill.

*   *   *

"These systems didn't work last time," she had urged while she and Ryder squared off in Osprey Point's laboratory.

The aging fluorescent bulbs flickered with the solar power illuminating the linoleum-lined floors and aisles of counters. The front lobby's door was closed, as was the door to the windowed conference room. The coldness of metal and glass waiting for scientific work usually pleased Satomi, but with doors closed and Ryder threatening to leave — the laboratory felt more like a prison than a sanctuary.

Satomi had seen it before — the terror of outbreaks in a large populace. Even though she hadn't entered the medical field at that time, she surmised any protocol short of complete isolation of healthy and complete extermination of the sick was no match for the infections that avalanched into cities. And even then.

"We know things we didn't know then. We're better prepared," had said ever-optimistic Ryder. "We will make it work. We have to make it work."

Ryder's supply of hair gel had finally been exhausted and her ash-brown hair was now being groomed into a flat pixie cut. Little silver rings lining her ears, pale pink skin, and an upturned nose validated Satomi's suspicions that Ryder was an otherworldly, mystical beauty. However, Ryder currently sounded more like a politician than any fey entity, combating reality with a determined positive attitude. Satomi expected her to stand on the counter and chant slogans at any moment.

Ryder had been nestled in Lysent Corp for the outbreaks. She didn't understand that the supposed cure had allowed survivors to regroup just to break down again, sending waves of infection out into the world. Ryder could remain optimistic, here at Osprey Point.

"You're not sick. Please just stay where you're safe," said Satomi, her dark eyes flashing darker under her tresses. "Dwyn is going. He's more than capable of caring for them."

Ryder shook her head, silver jewelry swaying underneath her ear.

"We don't know if Dwyn's cure will stick either," Ryder replied in a hushed tone as if speaking the possibility of failure at full volume made it more probable. Then more loudly, "but maybe you're the one that should be going — they need a doctor."

God, it was like talking to someone from a different world. On Ryder's planet, apparently the sick population she had irrevocably failed would welcome her continued medical expertise. In the real world, Satomi didn't even consider the possibility that Lysent's results were equally short-lived. No one had even heard rumor of reversion before Satomi's antivirals had been spread far and wide. And although it remained unspoken, Satomi knew they all blamed her. It was her fault. She knew it. They knew it. She had developed the temperature-stable antiviral. She had declared it safe and effective.

Satomi had doomed all the people in her community. The treated would turn, then consume. Precious Ryder would be torn apart by Satomi's deluded efforts to save the world. The defeated doctor settled in her stool and buried her head in a text book. A thick curtain of hair separated her from Ryder. Perhaps it would be easier if she couldn't watch it all fall away.

*   *   *

Satomi donned her jacket, but the goosebumps remained. She rubbed the offending extremities with her hands, but it wasn't just the cold wind or the wet dew on her bare feet. Her body was rebelling against her. Her head felt hot and stuffy, like it might explode. Nothing seemed in sync. Nothing made sense.

Satomi looked behind her toward the gate. The two figures standing on the scaffolding, watching for outside threats, ignored the threat that remained inside the fences. The one who had damned them all. Her eyes followed the chain links down to the sedans lining the inside of the fence. Rebar windows flashed in her mind and sent her stomach spiraling.

Satomi turned back around and tried to fight the rising tide inside her. Cold, damp air in her lungs to cool the frustration and shame. She would win against it, at least tonight she would. Satomi stared at the trailing cracks in the concrete and pretended she could count the invading blades of grass in the soft moonlight.

Some time later, Satomi caught sight of the sun peeking the tiniest pink rays, shadows on stars. She retreated back to her room, ducking into the darkest shadows, so no one would know her crime of sleeplessness. Her pant hem was soggy on the tile and back onto the carpet. She crawled into bed, which lay directly on the floor. The pillow pushed her long hair around her. It was wet from the morning and created a small cool environment around her racing mind. She imagined Ryder lying next to her; her soft skin pink with sleep. Satomi almost rolled over to caress the imaginary face before closing her eyes. Sleep was good. Ryder was good. She only wished she could be there, and not lost in the dew.

*   *   *

Satomi sat in the small two-room building that served as a mess hall and adjoining kitchen. An eclectic collection of tables, chairs, and benches had accrued in the space, but almost all were empty in the early morning hours. While Satomi hadn't been able to recognize the guards on the scaffolding in the darkness of late night, Branson and Tess had now been relieved from their shift and sat at a picnic table for a small meal before napping through the morning.

Branson's pearly brown hair was tied back with

elastic. His blue eyes twinkled with every laugh from Tess. Even sleep-deprived, they had no trouble keeping up with their constant flirting. Tess flicked her white blond hair off her shoulder, only for it to return again. While Satomi hadn't the energy to keep up with the latest gossip, it seemed Tess was still keeping Branson at arm's length, if only to protect her two young children from possible confusion and heartbreak.

Satomi appreciated their self-absorption. They made no mention of her nightly wandering and her subsequent status as a lump on a log. She tried to ignore the fact that they were sitting where Katie had lashed out at her weeks earlier. Katie's girlfriend Lisa had been the first to turn and attack her friends. Before Katie was sequestered at the motel for her own potential to revert, she had told Satomi it would have been better if she and Lisa hadn't been cured at all. They never would have found each other and lived in false hope.

Satomi wondered if Tess's and Branson's relationship and her own would suffer the same ends. Not wanting to be bothered with starting the communal fire, Satomi ate her serving of soupy grain corn and beans cold. Corn and beans weren't her favorite, but she knew they'd be eating foraged food before long. Watercress and mushrooms if they were lucky. Pine bark after that.

The mess hall door opened and someone took the long way around Satomi and her table. She hid underneath a frame of hair and eyed her half-full bowl. She couldn't just up and leave. Branson and Tess halted their banter.

"Hi," said the man, standing in front of her table,

hand on chair.

Another swallow of food. This one had a bit of crunch. Satomi looked up and stared at him without saying a word. An invitation to sit down wasn't coming. She understood having Pete Jr. — or Jack as they'd taken to calling him — stay was Osprey Point's best strategic play, but it didn't mean she and he needed to be on friendly terms.

Even if Satomi had stood up, Jack would still tower over her, his blue eyes constantly looking down to speak to others. In response to the dwindling supply of hair gel at Osprey Point, he had shaved his hair short — an odd decision as winter came rolling through. It emphasized the strong angles of his face, something he got from his father and had shared with his sister.

Jack and his family had controlled a hybridized infected army, brainwashed men with the resilience afforded to those sick with the z-virus. With their army lost to the Lysent Corporation, Osprey Point couldn't afford Jack joining Greenly's ranks. His potential to command the army under Greenly would secure Osprey Point's demise. Their only option was to welcome him into the fold. And he seemed to have a lot to contribute. However, he had also previously held Satomi captive for several months.

Jack held out a palm in half surrender. Satomi fought the urge to recoil. Without his leather armor, he was less intimidating, but she still connected his scent, his voice, and his mannerisms to the man who sat on a lawn chair throne and allowed his sister to be fiercely cruel to her and the community he now lived in.

"I'm sorry. With so many gone to the motel, I've only got so many people who will even acknowledge me…" he started.

Satomi wasn't surprised her cold stare was considered an acknowledgment. Jack and Jill had launched their army into Osprey Point upon first meeting. Satomi glanced over to Branson. His clenched jaw and vice grip on his spoon revealed he had not forgiven Jack for the death of a fellow guard, Lionel, during that proceeding.

"…My dad's refusing to eat. I'm at my wit's end," said Jack, his voice scratchy as if he too hadn't gotten much sleep.

"I'm not responsible for your father not eating. That's on you." Her voice tensed.

When she had first met Jack's father, Peter, she thought he suffered from some neurodegenerative disease. She worked to help him regain lost mental function until she learned he was involved in the development of the z-virus. He had manipulated the virus to create his army, and even his dementia had been triggered by one of his own experiments gone awry.

"Totally agree," he said hurriedly. "It's just he keeps asking about you… Evelyn and Eli too."

Sharp pain burned at the edges of her chest and throat at the mention of Eli's name. Her jaw clenched. Eli wouldn't be coming to see him. Jack's sister — Evelyn, Jill, whatever — had bled Eli out after he tried to protect her. Eli had been their loyal companion as they convoyed through the eastern states, and she killed him in anger. Shortly thereafter, Jill was killed by Larange Greenly's men.

"He'll forget. He always does." She brushed him off.

"No, he remembers you. And it doesn't help that Evelyn is gone. It's just me and he finds me boring."

Jack grinned.

Satomi wasn't sure what was funny.

Jack sighed, giving up on the humor. "You don't have to be OK with me. I get it. But my dad doesn't understand his circumstances. He just knows he's sad and he misses you."

The man was suffering. Given his hand in the global mass extinction, maybe he should. However, Satomi's responsibility as a doctor tapped her on the shoulder. Satomi sighed. More than clear ethics for medical care and experimentation, she wanted Jack out of her face.

"I'll think about it," she conceded.

Jack breathed a thanks and left the mess hall without breakfast.

"You don't owe him anything," Branson announced.

Satomi said nothing, her spoon scraping the sides of the bowl to finish her meal. Another unsettling crunch as she chewed. She didn't blame Peter one bit for refusing to eat this gruel.

CHAPTER THREE
QUARANTINE

Sunlight scattered through the skylights before Audra stirred. That stirring quickly brought to her attention an ache emanating from her tail bone. Cracked linoleum over concrete was not a forgiving surface. Audra assumed she'd be paying penance for the rest of the day. She arched her back and listened to the satisfying pops before twisting laterally for the same results. On her way around to her left, she glanced at the cot in Haleigh's and Eliza's cubicle. Just a small lump, barely moving the covers. A swath of dark hair peeked from the blanket's edge.

Audra stood up quietly and calculated the odds of being able to leave without argument. Haleigh's bag remained on the ground, half full. At least she hadn't continued packing. On top of the rotting cardboard box sat a thick sheet of handmade paper. Audra attributed its color and texture to food containers, something a grocery store would have in abundance. One side presented a monochromatic stick figure drawing. She turned the paper to find thinner ink, letters looping and curving. Haleigh's letter.

Audra averted her eyes. It was none of her business.

She pulled a large-mouth bottle from her bag and made sure no water still settled in it before she gently rolled the art for its protective sleeve. She did scan the contents of the box underneath the letter. Along with spare socks, a pair of eyeglasses, and the crayon she saw two more pieces of fruit leather. A jar of flour. And a cup of unshelled pecans.

This couldn't be everything. Some had been packed.

But still.

Audra wondered what they had traded for the paper. There was nothing else like it in the box.

"Mom said you could have another piece of fruit leather," Eliza's lilting voice escaped her rough blanket.

"Oh, no, I'm not hungry," Audra lied.

Straight arms protruded from the top of the blanket and came crashing down to the girl's sides, flipping the blanket off her face.

"Everyone's hungry."

Audra was almost sure that was true. Eliza was still younger than Audra was when the outbreaks occurred. She still remembered the oak dining room table, matching plates, and her mother's soft voice chiding her for spooning out more than she could consume.

"Where's your mom?" she asked. Surely Eliza wasn't left here by herself.

"Running. She has to do it now. Now that Kayle's gone." Of course she was left by herself. What else could her mother do? "Maybe Gordon could come and do the runs?"

Audra really hadn't dealt with such innocence and

youth in a long while. Not since Belinda, who although older, was more like a child than a supportive figure.

Eliza climbed off the cot. Her shirt rode up, too short for her thankfully growing body. She grabbed a dented tin pail and walked out.

She hadn't expected an answer.

Audra left as well, returning after trading a couple wares in her bag for a few days' rations. Neither of the space's occupants had returned. Audra wasn't sure how long this community's runs were. Could be hours, days, even weeks.

Audra slipped all the newly acquired food into the family's box. And after searching their bag, tucked her tent in its main pocket. How safe was leaving these things unattended? Audra scanned the produce section's population. Several older women huddled together on a mat, knitting and mending.

"Looking for someone?" a woman with wiry hair and an equally wiry voice asked.

"No, I have something for Haleigh and wasn't sure if I should leave it or just wait." Audra didn't even want to say it was food, although anyone could look into the box and know.

"Thieves don't last long here," the woman laughed, transferring her darning needle to her other hand before brandishing a butterfly blade.

Audra could find no reason to doubt her.

With her pack a little lighter, she abandoned Haleigh's cubicle. Bodies stopped and eyes stared as she headed toward the front of the store. They must not see too many venture out solo during the winter months.

The woman who patted her down was by the door

again.

Audra addressed her in a hushed voice.

"I'm not sure how this place is still here, but you need more guards on duty."

The woman cocked her head and raised her eyebrows at Audra.

Audra had a million other things to do before raiding a camp of families. "No seriously. Your cart wall out there is a flashing neon sign that people live here."

"That's how we trade, dear." The woman's condescending tone was clear.

Audra also had a million other things to do besides argue with a stranger over safety concerns. She promptly rolled her eyes and exited the damp grocery store.

Yesterday's overcast had been replaced with sunny coolness. Audra kicked herself for waking so late. It would throw off her entire journey. At least she didn't have a woman and her child clinging onto her legs, trying to prevent her escape.

Audra weaved her way through the maze, feeling the exterior guard's eyes on her back. When she reached the entrance, she marveled once more at the grocery cart wall. The bottom had been staked down deep. Ties and supports had been twisted through to keep them from toppling.

Use what you have, she guessed.

Still, she felt a little unsafe under its shadow. They were metal carts on wheels after all.

The edge of the asphalt crumbled as she stepped onto the faded road. Wide, sweeping cracks filled with tall weeds encouraged the deterioration. This main street once had a quiet life. Now it was even quieter.

The rusted gas station's pumps had been wrenched over. The pharmacy had been clearly raided many times over, its windows broken and nothing standing upright inside. The neighboring bank appeared untouched. Although maybe it was missing its chained pens and paper slips.

This was hardly a town. Why this chain grocery store had been placed here in all its magnificence was a mystery. And why it still stood now with just two guards taking most shifts was another. Not her problem, her mind recited. Still, she feared for Haleigh and her daughter.

Osprey Point and the quarantine location were south. Audra couldn't resist surveying the opposite direction. The road rambled into a fallen neighborhood of modular houses, and from there, fields.

Osprey Point south. North not.

Audra felt the pull. Almost like a panic. She wished for something else, anything else. And north was that.

If she returned to Osprey Point, she'd only watch her friends lose their last battles. Battles against the horrendous virus that had taken out so many. Family losing family. Friends. Lovers. She held Haleigh's and Eliza's correspondence in her bag, but she didn't need to read it to know it was just apologies, sadness, and regret. Eliza's drawing would just wrench the father's heart in two. It was better off undelivered. Their act of writing goodbye was for them — so they could move on.

What if Audra moved on?

Who would she find? Who could she be? Lost in the questions, not in the answers, Audra inhaled dry cold air and exhaled clouds of moisture. She stole another glance in the direction Osprey Point did not exist.

She would go there.

After Osprey Point's defenses fell and the quarantined consumed themselves, it would all be gone. She'd have no choice but to leave and never return. Current temptation be damned. The inevitability provided a certain amount of comfort.

She didn't have to go now.

She'd be going later.

She began her jog south, enjoying the tattered road to her temporary home.

*　　*　　*

With the safety of the light, and then the cover of darkness, Audra risked the roads back. She enjoyed the opportunity for straight, undeterred running. She flew through the day and far into the night, only stopping for watercress and accessible oyster mushrooms to fuel her. In her journey, she had purpose. She knew at her destination it wouldn't be so clear. So here, despite her race, she rested.

Audra took the overgrown exit ramp for a trucker's rest stop: a gas station and a motel for those who could no longer maintain their lane. The sun peeked over the pines — the time when drivers would leave motels like these, not arrive at them. She slowed to a jog as she turned the corner, giving a wave to the figure atop the gas station.

A quick-thinking resident had fenced the motel's parking lot when the outbreaks began; however, that hadn't saved its occupants from threats within. Soon zombies wandered freely inside. Audra had scouted out the motel many times before, as had many others. They had come to the same conclusion she had — clearing the parking lot, picking all the locks, and disabling everyone inside would be an intense feat.

But when Audra needed a place to separate their healthy from their potentially sick, it became necessary to finally clear the old motel of its zombie inhabitants — if only to replace them. And clearing wasn't nearly as difficult as convincing the previously infected to migrate the few miles from Osprey Point. It was an especially hard sell for those who had received their treatment from Lysent. She, like all the others, hoped Lysent was truthful in their claims that their antiviral was unaffected, but the risk was too great. Overlooking Lysent-cured could cause Osprey Point to fall like all the others.

Audra pulled on the heavy gate. It screeched, metal against concrete, like a rooster's strangled call just before the sun's arrival. She estimated the distance and slipped through the gap. Her pack caught on an aluminum barricade panel, sending it rattling in the cold air. So much for a quiet return.

Hushed voices paused as Audra made her entrance. The light hadn't quite slipped over the fences, but Audra saw a small wood fire going in the modified grill. It cast shadows on two women.

The parking lot held a few moldy chairs and rotting tables from select rooms, and scattered blue plastic water barrels. Audra smiled at the new addition — a metal picnic table, no doubt collecting dew. The two-story motel formed a U shape around the lot with each room's exterior doors facing the center.

Apparently recognizing but not acknowledging Audra, their voices started up again, heated and arguing. Audra recognized Ryder's sharp angles of ears and jewelry. Her petite figure with minute curves was also telling. Bradley's broad shoulders shook with emotion.

"I run high in the morning," Bradley pleaded.

"You didn't run high yesterday morning," retorted Ryder. Audra was surprised by Ryder's abrasiveness. Her diplomacy usually earned her few arguments.

"That's because I was up for a few hours before breakfast time. I just rolled out of bed. You can't take my temperature right after I roll out of bed…" Bradley trailed off, her voice souring. Perhaps she was realizing there was more than breakfast at stake.

"Good morning, what's up?" asked Audra, placing herself between the warring women. She ran her hands along her pack's straps before deciding to put it down.

"She has a temperature of a hundred-and-one," said Ryder coolly, washing the offending thermometer.

Bradley had journeyed toward Osprey Point alone when she was bitten. Audra found her just one mile off with a note in her pocket. Audra couldn't help but think she might need to write another note soon.

"And I'm telling her I always sleep hot. I'll cool down in a couple hours - well, unless you guys rile me up!" Bradley's face looked rosy, from her fever or anger Audra wasn't sure. But Bradley knew the protocol. Keep all doors closed. Temperatures taken every morning. Fevers stay in their rooms.

"A hundred-and-one doesn't sound like sleeping hot, Bradley," said Audra softly. "How do you feel?"

"Scared that you're going to lock me away because I came to breakfast too soon!" she shouted.

"OK, OK, look," said Audra, throwing up her hands in surrender. Tensions in the motel were high enough without people waking up to a yelling match. "It's just one reading. If you are sick — any kind of sick — maybe you shouldn't be out here. Get your breakfast and take it to your room. In a few hours, we'll take another temperature. No biggie. We just want you to be healthy and we want to keep germs — all the germs — to a minimum."

Bradley huffed but began picking her rations. Audra didn't address the fear in her eyes. Bradley just needed to come to terms with what was happening. The group didn't claim to know much about the reversion process, but Lisa had been sick for a few days before she turned and attacked people at Osprey Point. They hoped those were measurable symptoms heralding a reversion. It also could have been just a coincidence.

"How are things here?" asked Audra dumbly.

Ryder's narrow shoulders fell to an even sharper angle. The rising sun illuminated the bags under her eyes. She reached for a ring in her ear, spinning it around.

"Both Jia and Mary are sick, like bad sick. I think we're about to confirm the virus's reversion course. They were also the medical assistants. So now, all of this is on my and Gordon's shoulders."

And eventually Gordon would be gone too.

"Satomi?"

"She won't come. Also, she's better off trying to solve this from the lab. We're a lost cause here."

Ryder was far from the bubbly engineer who had hiked to an abandoned laboratory to save the world. Her optimism had fallen away to reveal someone very human. Ryder inspected her medical accoutrements, neatening their perfect rows along the table.

Audra couldn't draw up any words of comfort, just,

"I'll let Gordon know to run blood work on Bradley."

Pulling the bottle from her pack's main pocket, Audra didn't bother to take her bag to her room. Truth be told, she couldn't recall which room was hers at the moment. Instead, she climbed the concrete exterior stairs to the second floor. From there, the sun glared but didn't warm the air. It would be another cold night this evening. Audra knocked on the door marked 13. No one else had wanted the room. Gordon thought it seemed apt.

"Come in," came his distant voice, husky and muffled.

Finding the door unlocked, Audra opened it and flooded the room with soft light.

"Audra!" shouted Gordon, jumping from the small bucket where he was rinsing his face. "Did you find them?"

Gordon bounded over to her, his squared face wrinkling in both excitement and worry.

"Yes, yes I did —"

"Are they OK?" he asked before Audra could add anything to her answer.

Her nod yes sent his knees dropping to the floor. He was still almost as tall as Audra in that stance. His tawny skin matched the color of his thin-framed glasses, which turned askew as he pulled his large hands to his face. Audra unscrewed the canister and wiggled out the note. He immediately straightened his glasses, ready to receive the note, choking back tears.

Audra busied herself by pulling the curtains open as he read. All the rooms looked the same. Faded peeling floral wallpaper in greens and yellows. Defunct flat-screen TV. Dressers in various states of decay or destruction from their previous zombie tenants. Out of the corner of her eye, she saw Gordon's fingers run over the smoothness of his daughter's drawing.

"Are they safe there?" asked Gordon, not looking up from the drawing of his family together in a grocery store.

Audra waffled long enough for Gordon to turn his attention to her.

"What's wrong?" he asked, his voice deep.

Audra explained the scarcity of guards and Kayle's death. She also told him of the women who look after their section of the store, coloring them more as caregivers than knitters with knives. Honesty while not inciting Gordon into rushed action. Truth was, Haleigh and Eliza had survived this long without him. Audra was fairly certain they could continue to do so.

"Maybe they could live at Osprey Point? I could visit if just for a while." His half question, half wish hung in the air.

"They wanted to come see you," admitted Audra.

Audra had considered the option, but with Larange Greenly marking Osprey Point as the poster child for the rebellion, it was no safer than here. Best not to get them involved in any way.

Gordon's lips quivered with a small smile at her words. He frowned as Audra answered his question with a shake of her head. He didn't push the subject.

Audra hated to pull him back to reality, but duties remained. "Bradley had a fever this morning. We told her we'd check it again in two hours, but I imagine she'll need to be added to the list for regular blood work."

"Bradley. Got it," he replied with sad resolution.

CHAPTER FOUR
TURNED

When Audra exited Gordon's room, she noticed the sun had finally decided to grace the entire complex in light. She also noted that she was approaching twenty-four hours without sleep. A dull headache had settled in the back of her skull. She knew it would radiate upward the longer she stayed awake, until it wrapped around and impacted her vision. She would rest. Later.

Ryder was busy with breakfast screenings, trying to get temperatures before the early risers consumed hot beverages. Marcos appeared to have fallen back asleep on a half-padded chair. It was difficult to tell with the waves of rich black hair that framed and often covered his face. Audra joined the tiny mob around the grill and managed a generic motel mug filled with pine needle tea and a scratchy blanket that had been warmed by the fire. Initially Audra hadn't been sold on the motel, but its amenities were surprisingly helpful.

With more people awake, the gate didn't sound quite as loud as Audra slipped out with her sights on the gas station. Audra had worried their location was too close to the highway. And really, it was. But the neighboring gas and convenience store with its flat roof had convinced her security could be manageable.

When she and Dwyn were scouting and first climbed up the metal cage surrounding the ladder and reached the pea gravel roof, the space felt oddly vacant and even otherworldly. It had taken a moment for Audra to realize why.

The space was untouched.

The interior of the gas station had been raided several times over just as the rest of the world. But the roof had remained a spot the end hadn't touched. The last person up there had been experiencing a different universe. Maybe his biggest concern was greasing a stuck vent. In his world, the sick didn't walk around and consume their brethren. The sick stayed home, ate soup, and watched TV.

Undisturbed as the world fell, places like this had become rare.

And Audra thought most unfortunate.

An unused resource was a reminder that someone else hadn't made it to that point. Perhaps if the roof had been more accessible, someone could have escaped a herd. They could have enjoyed a few more quiet nights with a warm fire and a chance to gaze at the stars. Instead, the unmarked roof showed no history of campfires and the gravel remained unfussed. Anyone nearby had found another means of evasion or had been overrun.

The roof was an excellent watch spot. From the vantage point, Audra and Dwyn could see inside the motel's fences, its gate, the highway, and both ramps.

"This will do," Audra had said.

And finally the resource was used.

Having found the key to the ladder inside the gas station, it was now easy to traverse to the top. Audra managed the metal rungs one-handed. Her peace offering was in the other hand. The roof was still a mostly empty and serene place, but now the white gravel had been marked up with campfires, and some weather-resistant odds and ends were scattered about.

Wisps of chestnut brown hair peeked out of a bundled blanket wrapped tightly around curves. On a birch log by the fire, Katie sat on guard. Audra offered the white ceramic mug and the woman's knobby hand emerged from cloth to receive it. She pulled the tea close and let the steam warm her face. Katie, like everyone in quarantine, drank copious amounts of pine needle tea, hoping its vitamin C would ward off any illness. Audra draped the second blanket over Katie's shoulders, which fell gently with the added weight.

Audra sat on a milk crate next to her. The road and forest were quiet. It seemed the birds and few small animals left in the area were sleeping in. Audra cleared her throat and asked the obligatory question.

"How's Lisa?"

Lisa had sent Audra into a panic on two separate occasions. The first was their meeting, when Audra stumbled upon her in the woods. Infected, yellow blond hair, and formerly blue eyes — wandering, lost in the world, she looked just like Audra's sister Belinda. Audra had brought her in as their first outreach and cure. Then later, she was the first to revert. She infected three other people before Audra contained her.

"In pain," she said, exasperated.

The infection was not a passive thing. Those cured recounted sensations of burning bones and joints that sent shocks of pain with each degree of rotation.

"Sometimes I wish I'd go ahead and revert. Join her. Maybe time would pass more quickly." Katie tipped her cup and watched some of her tea pour out onto the roof.

So much for her peace offering. Katie's eyes shot daggers at her. And Audra was out of platitudes, having given them all to Gordon. She had already promised them hope when she brought them to Osprey Point. She couldn't promise again at the motel.

Audra knew her frustration. She had carried it and the accompanying guilt for years. Your loved one rots in pain. Your progress to save them excruciatingly slow. And some days, you don't even bother. And that's the scary part. Katie watched her girlfriend revert and infect others, somehow not getting caught in the scuffle. And now she had nothing to do but perform her guard duties and wait for her dormant virus to take hold. Idle and emotional hands.

After a few moments of foggy silence, Audra stood up to leave.

She would go check the snares. A dinner of meat would improve morale. It always did, until the residents remembered flesh-eating conversion. Then the game wouldn't settle as well in their stomachs. And their minds would churn as well.

But Audra had nothing else to do either.

*　　*　　*

If Audra had been more clear-thinking, she might have realized speaking with Katie in both their sleep-deprived states would be counterproductive. But, Audra didn't plan to stay at the motel long. And she knew if she delayed the meeting, she'd find a way to leave before it occurred.

Audra promised herself sleep. After she checked the snares.

The cool air dulled the forest smells, but the expanse still felt isolating and peaceful. She knew Katie was watching her from above. Probably pouring out the rest of her tea. But it didn't matter, Audra would be deep in the woods soon. Her figure fading into pines and oaks.

Four snares then sleep.

Noise at the first snare did not sound like the flailing of a delicious animal. It sounded like a dumb human.

Not another.

But when she approached the area, she recognized Dwyn's height, his dark curly hair flying in multiple directions. He turned, surprised, then a large toothy grin expanded over his face.

"I thought I'd check them for you. Figured you'd be asleep."

"No, the snares are my job," she said curtly, communicating her displeasure.

His dimples disappeared with his grin. He dug his toe into the ground, submitting to her.

If the last twenty minutes had been a bad time to interact with others, these minutes would be worse. She hadn't meant to be rude in her greeting; she had just hoped to be alone out here. She hadn't even seen him enter the woods.

"You don't have to take it all on your shoulders, you know."

While she deserved a rebuke, there was much more kindness in it than Audra was comfortable with. She knew he meant more than the snares. It's what Haleigh had said about Gordon.

No one should do this alone.

Audra bit her tongue and instead of replying, started to the next snare. She neither encouraged nor discouraged his following.

He followed as she knew he would.

The next was up over the hill. Her boots treaded softly on the dank pine needles, the crunch of the amber needles gone with fall. Dwyn's footsteps followed almost as muted. No words between them, she could dismiss his noises as a zombie following her climb. She followed the ridge of the landscape, the dry breeze making her face feel tight. Her headache rumbled toward the crown of her head.

Audra had done it alone for so long. Even when she'd carried her sister, she was alone.

A gust of wind grabbed at her hair and continued over the edge and into the valley, swaying the brush and small trees. It wasn't difficult for Audra to imagine the movement in the woods below as that of the dead, drifting like sea currents over the earth. An ocean of hands and teeth.

So many gone. And yet, someone was still to be last.

Maybe chance would choose her. Maybe she was destined to do it alone.

Then, she'd stand last. Until she decided not to. She'd lift the burden from her shoulders and chase it into the sea. She'd leave the world to its fate. Devoid of higher humans. Devoid of higher purpose.

Dwyn and Haleigh were right.

No one could do it alone. Least of all, she.

"Who is that?" called Dwyn behind her.

As if her thoughts had conjured him, a figure climbed the hill towards them. He scrambled uncoordinated, but in using all four of his extremities, he would cover the distance in short time.

Audra held out her hand in caution. Dwyn's curiosity always got the best of him. He'd be stutter-stepping down to meet the danger head-on. She wasn't sure what it was yet, much less who.

This far from Osprey Point's perimeter, roaming rotters were more common, but the thing scaling the hill was more man than rot. Arms, legs, torso, and neck all held proper angles. Well-preserved, not even weather-torn, he could be a half zom scout with many brethren to come. Audra looked past him into the valley and beyond, fearful for a second that her sea of death wasn't a dream. Nothing of the sort. For now.

As he pulled himself up to Audra's and Dwyn's level, Audra recognized the slack-jawed demeanor of a freshly turned, but full-fledged zombie.

And it was just a kid.

Audra sidestepped as she inspected him. No scruff on his paling face. Ash brown hair fell to his shoulders. He was fourteen, fifteen tops. A thin arm reached toward them, its hand ripped open by teeth and now filled with brambles from his climb. He let out a snarl from the corner of his mouth. Audra tried to recall where she knew him from.

She pictured him with shorter hair that didn't cover the green eyes or the freckled cheeks.

"Kip," she said. The zom's head jerked in her direction. More likely in response to the sound than his name.

"He lives in Uno. Or, did."

Uno was the last township on the Lysent rail line. Kip had approached her a few years ago, even more so a kid. He asked her to teach him how to tag. Audra told him no. Told him if he lived in the townships and didn't need to cure a loved one, he should just count his blessings and stay home.

He should have stayed home.

"Help me leash him so we can get him back."

"To Uno?" asked Dwyn.

Audra looked around and realized she didn't have her pack. She had left it at the motel. Her headache shot a bolt of lightning between her eyes. She wouldn't be able to get him back to Uno today. He'd have to come with them.

"Home first. Do you have anything we can tie him up with?"

"What if Uno doesn't want him?"

Dwyn had a point. Even if the corporate cures worked, getting them had become near impossible and a null point. People could barely afford food, much less the treatment for someone who would also need to eat during the winter months and beyond.

And did the corporate cures work? Audra didn't want to think about it. Didn't need to think about it. She would return Kip to his responsible party. They could decide his fate. This was finally a decision Audra didn't have to make.

Audra pulled some dying vine off a tree. Dwyn hadn't offered anything of value.

"That will cut into his wrists," said Dwyn.

What the hell did it matter? Despite it not being her decision, she guessed he'd never be cured. She didn't reply.

Dwyn got behind and held the boy's arms straight out. Audra bound them together.

"What do you think he's doing out here?" asked Dwyn.

"You mean, what *was* he doing out here," corrected Audra. She reached into the boy's coat pockets.

"That's stealing," explained Dwyn.

"Maybe it will tell us why he's out here. Or, maybe he has a snack to share with us, since we're being so kind to travel with him."

Dwyn shook his head, but didn't argue.

Audra pulled a folded paper from his back pocket. It was machine-pressed, not something a teenager in a Lysent-outskirting town would typically possess. Perhaps he was delivering a letter? Her face crinkled as she scanned its contents.

"What does it say?" asked Dwyn, his curiosity winning over any thoughts of keeping the zom under control.

Audra gave it a hard kick in the back and it tumbled halfway down the hill. It would take time for it to come back up.

"Hey, be gentle," reprimanded Dwyn.

"Hell with that," said Audra as she shoved the letter into Dwyn's chest and slumped against a ragged pine tree, watching their zom climb back up on feet and elbows.

Dwyn read over the form.

"I don't get it," he said. "They're looking for zombies?"

"It's a bounty list offered by Lysent. It's got tag numbers, names, and last-known locations. A hundred and fifty credits redeemable for fuel and food per head."

"So, he's a —"

"Tagger." Kip had apparently gotten his wish. "Check out the name at the bottom of the list."

"Yours. Gordon's on here too."

"Along with half of Osprey point," added Audra. "I recognize all the names. They're looking for MY zombies."

"But they're not all zombies."

"No, but Lysent could make the argument that they were all given faulty cures and will turn."

Audra picked up a stick and dug it into the soft dark ground, spinning it in a screwing motion.

"But why?"

"Who knows," she said. But she knew. Greenly had her army. And she wasn't content to just go in for the kill. First, she'd destroy everything around Audra. She would hurt anyone Audra had ever interacted with. And after Audra watched everything burn, Greenly would grow bored like a cat playing with a mouse — and she'd either end Audra's life or worse, not.

Alone. The last.

Kip arrived back to them.

"What are you going to do with him?" worried Dwyn. Audra threw the stick in her hand. The zombie lurched, following the motion like a dog. The idea this young man could capture anyone seemed laughable, but Audra knew there would be more capable opportunists. "Are you taking him back to the township?"

"No, who's to say they won't grab me and turn me in."

"I could take him."

"He was going to turn us in for cash! He doesn't deserve to go home. He deserves what he got."

"None of us deserve this."

And Audra knew he believed that. But she wasn't convinced that she didn't deserve it. What did she think was going to happen when she took on Larange

Greenly and her massive corporation? She should've minded her own damn business. Now, lots of people were going to get hurt.

Audra fought the urge to kick Kip again. Instead she stood up and took a less-steep route back to the motel. Kip and Dwyn followed, other snares forgotten.

CHAPTER FIVE
RESTITUTION

Satomi walked past her room, no longer feeling the high anxiety that had led her to flee earlier that morning. Her eyes flitted from the carpet's worn and blurred geometric patterns to the two tin mugs of liquid she balanced. Peter's room was farther down the hall and to the right.

Jack hadn't even formally given his request during their conversation when Satomi had decided to visit Peter. He was the one person who didn't know what awful things she had done — the false hope she had shared. He didn't even know what awful things he had done. The death toll was in the billions.

His door had a chain installed on its exterior to keep him from wandering. Satomi used one hand and arm to hold the cups of pine needle tea, and the other hand to pull the chain as discreetly as she could before knocking. Satomi was uncertain if Peter remembered or even knew about the chain. She certainly didn't want to explain it.

She gave three firm knocks and listened to the long

session of shuffling behind the door. If he took a while it was due to confusion, not physical limitations. Soon, the door opened a crack and its owner didn't even peer out to identify the caller.

"I don't want any food, thank you."

"How about a friend, then?" she asked.

Peter let the door open to a wider angle. His silver hair was combed and parted. He wore a denim shirt tucked into his denim jeans. A neat black belt separated the two. Satomi gave a smile and Peter's blue eyes brightened.

"Evelyn!" he said as he swooped in for a hug, his arms under hers. Satomi held the teas out at length to avoid burning him or herself.

"Satomi, remember?" she said into his ear, her chin resting on his neck. He pulled back immediately, another jostle to her frame and to the teas. He stared hard into her face. His brow furrowed and she wondered if he might throw a tantrum.

"That's what I said," he said. He welcomed her inside.

His room was a poor substitute for the studio apartment on wheels Jack had built him. A straw mattress much like hers, sat in one corner of the room. A table and chairs were the only real furniture. An interior office meant no windows. Along the wall stood a stack of books. Peter spent a lot of time reading.

"Tea, tea," he said, looking around his room. There was no stove to make tea.

"I brought tea," she said as she placed it on the wood veneer table and motioned for him to sit down.

"Oh yes, of course," he mumbled. He sat down, folded his hands in his lap, and waited. He cut his eyes at her. Satomi was sure he had forgotten who she was, but she wasn't sure if it was momentary or if Jack had brought her here under false pretenses.

Satomi slid the cup across the table to Peter. Satomi liked her tea strong and unsweetened, which worked well in the new world of pine trees and dandelion roots. She had resorted to stealing honey from Ryder's stash to temper the tea's sharp taste for Peter. He sipped it and smiled up at her at its sweetness.

Satomi sat across from him and shared his smile. It was easy to like Peter and almost impossible to reconcile the meek and pleasant personality with the person who created a slave army. Satomi wished she knew the truth about his character. If he gained additional mental function, would he be a different person?

"What are you up to, today?" he asked jovially.

"Oh, work, you know."

In truth, probably fumbling around in the laboratory, pretending she had even the first clue how to save her friends from a terrible disease. Her chest tightened at the thought. Helplessness and stress were not benefactors to Eureka moments. And she needed a big one if she was ever going to make progress.

"What kind of work do you do?" he asked.

"I'm a doctor… well, a scientist I guess, at the moment," she stumbled through her words. She wasn't sure if being honest was a good idea but she found a need to talk to someone. She guessed she hadn't much gotten the chance with Ryder being out.

"Oh, I'm a scientist too!" Peter said, his chest puffing a bit. "It's a very noble field."

Satomi couldn't suppress her eyebrow raise, but she did offer a small smile.

"I work with nasty bugger viruses," he started. "Research and development — can you believe that? We actually develop viruses."

"That sounds dangerous," led Satomi.

Working with the original z-virus, he must have some insight. Did his broken mind hold the key to her Eureka moment?

"Yeah, well, I figure it's better to have a finger in the pie. It's my only chance to know what's going on. I don't want to get stuck in the crossfire."

Billions dead.

While it was unfair to blame a middle-management scientist for Lysent's fatal direction, he had realized the risks in his work. Satomi couldn't be sure of the end result if she returned Peter to his former glory in his 'noble field'. But for now, other matters were easier to settle.

"Speaking of pie, I hear you're not eating, Peter."

"Do you have pie?" he asked, looking up from his cup.

Satomi laughed at her mistake. She didn't know anyone who wouldn't be happy to eat a sweet, buttery pie right now. "No, I'm sorry."

"You know they don't feed me," he announced.

His face settled into a worried almost fearful look, as if he really was having trouble getting people to feed him. Satomi imagined his current hunger might be enforcing these thoughts. Did old Peter assume the role of a victim too? Did he ascribe his awful choices to just trying to keep his family alive and well?

"That's awful. If I go get you some food, will you eat it?" she asked.

"Oh yes, thank you. I'm really quite hungry," he said, and smiled.

Satomi wasn't sure what her punishment should be for failing in her antiviral work, but this was definitely Peter's restitution. He had a great mind and little access to it. He had become a burden to the son he was trying to save. Lost a daughter and couldn't mourn her. If Satomi could release him from this mental purgatory, would he deliver the remaining population from his past sins or would he continue to pull strings for personal gain?

Peter's eyes swept over the dreary, windowless room. "Also, I'd like to go home."

Satomi nodded. She gathered the empty cups and promised to return with food for her friend.

*   *   *

Finally feeling tired, Satomi purposefully marched past her room after successfully getting Peter to eat. If everyone else was kind enough to not mention her insomnia, she would also pretend it didn't exist. She walked through the plaza, around the fountain where people mingled, chatting and laughing Since the previously cured had been sequestered, Osprey Point had become guiltily relaxed.

Satomi walked through the laboratory's lobby, which now only contained some spare medical equipment and a tremendous pile of telephone cords tangled in a corner. The dark paneling on the walls remained, but desk, chairs, and even waiting area reading materials had been usurped by other community residents.

On the other side of the door lay the reason they were here at Osprey Point. Vesna had helped them locate this isolated laboratory forgotten by Lysent

Corporation. It had seemed like a gold mine with its lab equipment and scientists to cure and recruit.

Now, it sat empty. Everyone but Satomi sent to quarantine.

Sure, the equipment was still there. Three rows of counters with cabinet space underneath. Refrigerators against the back wall. Microscopes sat uniformly in a line. Beakers and notebooks scattered with a day's work before its scientists were ushered to a motel. With these items and any available solar power, Satomi was supposed to prevent the extinction of the human race.

Satomi had pushed them to swap the populations. Let those not at risk for reversion go to the motel. They'd have a larger population of scientists working in the appropriate space. But, it was decided the laboratory itself was too valuable for it to be lost in an outbreak. No, Satomi would remain.

Remain to do what, she wasn't sure.

Since she had let go of First, do no harm, decisions had become difficult. Now she was plagued with questions as to what the right direction was. She thought when she saved Ryder from that zombie and held her close that everything would fall into place, but it hadn't.

Ryder refused to stay where she was safe.

Peter didn't deserve to be cured.

Osprey Point depended on her to work diligently in her laboratory until she stepped out with a vial of miracles. Instead, Satomi sat on a stool and stared at an empty space on the counter. She didn't have the slightest clue what was wrong with the antiviral.

A noise behind her startled her. Satomi gave a little yip before turning around to see.

"Sorry to surprise you," said Marla, poking her head in before entering completely into the laboratory. She pushed her black-framed glasses higher onto her nose, which was softly freckled. "I just wanted to see if I could help you today."

Marla was Ryder's junior engineer. She hadn't any formal education, but she did have a knack for figuring out how to fix things. Ryder had taken her under her wing and taught her engineering principles. Together, they were building the infrastructure for a better Osprey Point. Satomi could only wish her work were as tangible as theirs.

"No… no," Satomi hesitated. She wasn't sure what she was doing, much less what someone else would do to help her.

Marla sat down on the stool next to Satomi. She leaned with her hands on the seat between her legs. She looked to Satomi earnestly, sprigs of red hair tucked behind her ears.

"I know it sucks we're all separated," she said. "But, once we figure this out, we'll be able to reunite with everyone."

Once *I* figure this out… Satomi knew she meant well, but this wasn't helping. Just a reminder of the stakes that were avalanching on top of her, paralyzing her.

"Maybe if you explained to me what you were working on, something might come to you?" Marla suggested.

Satomi shook her head. "I could use more fuel, though. I can't get my materials hot enough with the solar energy."

Marla nodded eagerly, jumping off the stool, believing Satomi's lie. With her exit, Satomi suddenly missed her presence. Unhappy with people. Unhappy without.

Satomi opened her composition notebook and looked over the numbers again, hoping they would offer her some hidden insight on the thousandth viewing. She had measured the viral load in the patients she treated for the z-virus. With each treatment, the load decreased until it wasn't measurable. Then, she continued to test for over a month, to ensure the virus was eradicated from the person.

But the blood sample from Lisa showed the virus had burgeoned in her body. It had not only been reintroduced into her system; it had come back with a vengeance. The viral load was so massive, the three people she bit turned almost immediately.

The virus's return reminded Satomi of bacteria developing resistance to the drugs used to combat them. If this was simply acquired resistance, treating those who hadn't been previously cured should also become more difficult, but it hadn't. And besides the viral load, she saw no difference between first and second infections. She was missing something.

Something that Peter might know. But was it fair to spend precious time curing the person who had put the world in this predicament? Could he fix what he had broken? Peter might just make things worse.

Satomi wished Eli were here to help her decide, or at least keep her company. While he had helped keep her prisoner — standing large at the door of Peter's mobile lab — he was a good man. Despite not having a foundation in science, he was curious and always gave her his undivided attention as she spoke. His warm smile would make his russet face glow, especially when he comprehended a concept Satomi was explaining. He had died protecting her from Jill. To save Peter, her father, felt like betraying Eli.

Eli wasn't here… maybe that was her fault.

Satomi pushed the notebook to the back of the counter. She bent at the waist and let her forehead touch the cool vinyl counter. Her hair fell down at all sides and created a small space of darkness.

She wished to be gone like Eli.

CHAPTER SIX
STRATEGY

The morning had gotten late. Audra knew those allowed to be outside their rooms would be when they arrived. Audra grabbed a handful of the back of Kip's shirt as Dwyn wrenched the gate open. Everyone stopped what they were doing and stared at the two's prize.

Katie leaned over a water barrel marked 'Laundry'. Apparently, sleep was escaping her as well. Marcos was fully awake, splitting wood in the far corner. Several others were eating breakfast or otherwise keeping busy in the daylight.

"Who is that?" asked Ryder. She rose from a table scattered with tools and broken contraptions.

"Someone from Uno. He followed us home."

"Then let Uno take care of him," Katie called over.

Kip purred at the sight and scent of Ryder approaching. Her eyes were wide and her voice was hushed. "I don't think this is a good idea."

"He can't go back to Uno. I'll explain later. But this *is* quarantine. And he needs *quarantining*." Audra wasn't sure what the big deal was.

"It's just… these people don't need reminders of what they're struggling with." She eyed the young man, pulling like a junkyard dog, t-shirt stretching. "This guy lived in Lysent towns? Let them deal with him. We've got our own to care for. This is bad for morale. You're not here all the time. You don't realize how delicate these people are."

Audra really didn't give a shit how delicate they were. They were turning their backs on a form they were destined to inhabit. If they had red expiration dates stuck onto their foreheads, they'd read 'tomorrow' and 'past due'. They could easily be the next on a leash, foaming at the mouth.

Audra pushed Kip through the parking lot. If anyone had a problem with it, they'd have a physical fight on their hands.

"This is ridiculous. We don't want him here," said someone from the picnic table.

It took a moment for Audra to locate him since he didn't have the courage to meet her eye. It didn't matter. They all needed to hear it.

"What you don't understand is he is you."

Audra scooped up her bag. She wasn't going to pitch a fit over where Kip would stay. He could stay with her. Kip tripped on the curb, slowing their departure. Audra hoped it wouldn't dull the sting of her last words.

They were pretty good last words.

Once inside her room, she walked Kip over the low-pile carpet and released him into the bathroom. Closing the door, she pressed her forehead on it for a moment, listening to the teenager wander the small space. She wouldn't abandon him.

She had done enough of that.

* * *

After blessed sleep in which Audra was sure she hadn't stirred a bit since falling face first into the mattress, she woke to fumbling noises in the bathroom. The light bordering her curtains told her it was evening. Audra wondered which evening.

Wiping the sleep from her eyes, she checked her pack for anything needing to be replenished or replaced. She would need extra rope. And she'd need food, but that still wasn't something she was willing to take from the motel.

After washing with a rag and bucket, Audra put on the spare clothes from her bag. Her jacket on top of that. She balled up clothes to take across the way to wash. Resisting the urge to say goodbye to Kip, she stepped outside. Her skin, being recently wet, prickled with the cold underneath her loose clothes.

Dusk was well on its way. The sky was pink with streaks of gray clouds. People were eating supper before the sun dipped and left them in the dark. Audra washed her clothes in the laundry basin and silently waited for the majority of the residents to retire to their rooms. She wanted to meet with the core group, and didn't want the whole motel butting in.

After hanging up her articles of clothing to dry, and hopefully not freeze in the night's air, she invited Dwyn, Gordon, Ryder, and Marcos to meet in her motel room.

Marcos and Gordon brought their own chairs of wood and worn padding in. They sat along the round table with Dwyn. On the bed nearby, Ryder sat with legs crossed and feet tucked under. Audra joined her. Despite their disagreements, they could still remain amiable.

Each had brought in an LED or lantern with homemade fuel (thanks to Ryder's engineering skills) which created patches of light on the wallpapered walls and on the serious faces of the group.

"Should I let Kip out to join the meeting?" Audra teased. Everyone shook their heads 'no,' in case she planned to push the joke further.

They knew her too well.

"Dwyn says there's a list?" asked Marcos.

Without ceremony, Audra pulled out the Lysent directive. They all took turns reading it under their light of choice.

"It's safe to say Lysent is trying to draw you out," announced Ryder, her arms resting on her crossed legs. She glanced at Audra's bag, which was not unpacked. "Are you going to be drawn out?"

"I don't see how I can not go. They're my tags. If I don't help them, no one will."

"A lot of these names are here at the motel," Dwyn reminded softly. "You're not responsible for everyone on this list. You're on this list too, y'know. You need to stay safe."

"The people here are safe. Everyone still thinks this place is overrun. It's the people I left behind. I need to help them."

Ryder shook her head in disagreement.

"I'll go too then," said Dwyn. Audra knew he would offer.

"No, I need you to go to Lysent."

"Wait, what?" he asked, taken aback.

"We don't know if the corporate cures are working.

We don't know what she plans to do with her half-zom army. We're in the dark here."

"And how am I supposed to shed light on any of that?"

Audra stopped pulling on a snagged string on her bed's blanket, and mustered the courage. "Corette."

"What! Corette doesn't want to see me!" His face balled up in confusion or pain. "She refused to see me when I was cured. She doesn't want anything to do with me."

Corette and Dwyn were engaged when the outbreaks started. They survived together until Dwyn was bitten. Corette eventually found Lysent, married another, and was able to pay for Dwyn's treatment.

"You really don't get it, do you?" asked Audra.

The wrinkles atop the bridge of Dwyn's nose remained as he tried to decipher her meaning. The others waited awkwardly. Audra was sure some of them had figured it out as well. She hated having this conversation with Dwyn in a group setting, but she wasn't sure if she'd have the guts to tell him otherwise.

"She married him so she could awaken you! She doesn't hate you. She loves you."

Audra's love for Belinda had led Audra to signing her life to the only entity that claimed a successful awakening process. Audra was sure Corette had also signed her life away to save the person she loved. And she signed it with an 'I do.'

Despite the overall shades of jealousy Audra felt for Corette's successes where Audra had failed, Corette could have connections who would be able to give them critical information — attack plans, virus protocols, or more.

"You're grasping at straws," he said with more than

a touch of bitterness.

"We need all the straws we can get," said Audra.

And she knew they weren't straws.

Vesna had protected many secrets in her life, but in one instance she hinted that Dwyn had a second connection to the rebel network. When he finally spilled his story months ago, Audra understood.

"I wouldn't even know how to contact her."

"Rosie can connect you. She'll know. She handles all the awakening accounts."

Rosie worked the front desk in Lysent's main building. She was the first person you saw, and as Audra had heard from reports, was still the first person, despite having helped Audra. She had kept Belinda safe from being executed with Vesna by never submitting Audra's release request. She then warned Audra about the impending attack on the laboratory.

Pain shadowed on Dwyn's face. It was obvious he still loved Corette and didn't appreciate the ripping open of an old wound in the name of reconnaissance. But, they were in desperate need for any sort of advantage. Without it, they'd die. And if Greenly was lying about the efficacy of Lysent-sponsored treatment, lots of others would die too.

"OK. I will talk to her if she will see me," he said as he gave in.

When Audra heard those words, a sharp pain glanced her heart. Images of Dwyn and another girl flashed in her mind. All of a sudden Audra wasn't sure if she had won or not. But it did not matter. Only her people mattered. Not her. Not her vacillating feelings for the annoying man she refused to call Wilfred.

"I'm on the list," said Gordon as if everyone else had missed it.

"Yes, I'm sorry about that," Audra mumbled.

When Gordon had first started looking for his family, Audra had scanned his DNA with her biometric reader. It hadn't told them much, just that someone at some time had inquired about him. Big whoop. However, it had also transmitted the information to Lysent Corporation as the reader was company property. Just another tentacle of the ever-reaching company.

"Don't be. I'm worth food and fuel."

"You're worth credits," she corrected. "Lysent controls the pricing of food and fuel. They could call inflation or whatever the hell they wanted and say you're worth one night's meal."

"That's one more night. Promise me. When I turn, you'll surrender me to Lysent and give the bounty reward to my family." Audra balked. "It's the only way I can provide for my family now."

Audra chewed on her lip. She knew she'd have done the same for Belinda.

Even if she was worth just one night's meal.

Gordon couldn't let Haleigh and Eliza go hungry or be cold, especially if he was mindlessly wandering a remote location as he had for years before.

"OK, I promise," she declared, releasing her bottom lip. Although Audra knew if she could provide for his family another way, there'd be no need to surrender his body to the cold marbled building that was Lysent.

"Ryder, Marcos, keep them safe here. Forage, but don't go far. I don't want anyone getting snagged by a tagger."

"I still don't understand why Lysent wants us — me," said Marcos.

"We live outside their system. Lysent thinks we're a threat. And hopefully we are. Any word from Satomi?" asked Audra.

"No," said Ryder. "And we haven't figured it out here either."

Another reason Audra should leave. She couldn't help them here, but she might be able to outside their fences.

"Things are going to get bad… real bad, before it gets better," said Gordon.

And they might not get better. But moping in a candlelit seance circle wasn't going to get them anywhere. They hugged and said their goodbyes in the small calm before the storm.

CHAPTER SEVEN
GOODBYE

Dwyn slept on the second floor with his curtain open, so he'd wake with the rising sun. He knew Audra would be getting an early start. She wouldn't stay for goodbyes. He'd have to be outside and in her way to see her off.

His heart had beaten heavily in his chest at the mention of Corette's name from Audra's lips. Worlds colliding. Corette's name stirred a firestorm of pain and confusion. When he was bitten and the virus coursed through his body, all he felt was pain. Then, he suddenly awakened to find he couldn't return to anything he knew. Anything he loved. Corette refused to see him. While Audra ran as a means to escape, Dwyn started running and working for Vesna to fill his life with — something.

Then, he found Audra. A woman who didn't put up with shit in a world full of shit. While his heart involuntarily fluttered in every moment they shared, more than a romantic relationship, he wanted Audra to feel comfortable around the people she defended so intensely. She built a community. Two communities. And refused to live in either one.

The picnic table felt like ice on his rear as he waited for Audra in the morning chill. Could she be right? Corette had married to cure him, not because she loved another?

It was presumptuous.

It was nice to think about.

Even if Audra wasn't correct, she still had a point. Corette at least had felt obligated to make sure he didn't rot in that sedan. If he could speak with her, maybe she'd be willing to share some information that would avert disaster. Or at least, let them know when and what was coming.

Audra looked surprised when she stepped out of Room 2, her pack already on her back.

"You didn't think you'd be able to leave without saying goodbye, did you?"

"One could only hope…" she replied.

It was always difficult to know when she was joking.

Dwyn's knees popped as he got up from the cold seat. While he hadn't aged much during his infection, it still seemed to be catching up to him. He thrust out a bag of shelled pecans, dried fruit, and oatmeal bars with a straight arm to signal his determination that she have it.

"I'm not taking from the stores. They need it here. I can find food while I'm out there."

"Please take it just in case you run into trouble. It's not from the stores. I gathered it while you were sleeping yesterday," he lied.

Fortunately, Audra took the bag without looking at its contents. She shoved it in a side pocket of her pack. Still not saying goodbye long enough to take her pack off. They both walked to the gate.

"And trouble? When have I ever gotten into trouble?" she asked and smiled.

"Only every time you run headstrong into it. So just don't, this one time," he grimaced.

"I'll see how I'm feeling," she said and shrugged with a smile. She was joking this time. Maybe.

Audra tucked her arms underneath his and snuggled her face into the layers of corduroy and flannel on his chest. He kissed her softly on the top of her head. If they could be like this forever, that would be OK. Better would be Audra stopping for just a moment to realize she didn't need to go running off to save people who had never known her, just because Greenly had put them on a list.

He opened the gate for her and she was gone.

Dwyn trudged back to his room to begin packing for his trip. He hadn't done it the night before, because the temptation to help Audra tag would have been too much. It would have been like old times, running maneuvers in the woods and fields, branches and teeth snapping.

*   *   *

By the time Dwyn had prepped his bag and stepped out of his dim quarters, the place was bustling with people. Most of them were lined up to get their temperatures taken so they could line up again to get breakfast. The door next to him opened and Gordon emerged from his own poorly lit accommodations.

"Morning — where you going?" Dwyn asked, eying Gordon's khaki-colored pack.

"With you," he said with a smile.

"I appreciate it, Gordon. But they need you here."

"Nah, they don't. Ryder's pretty good at drawing and testing blood now. Marcos is organizing the food-gathering trips."

"I still think you can do more here," suggested Dwyn. It wasn't that he didn't want the company… "I'm probably just headed for a dead end."

"You and me both, brother." He gave Dwyn a small punch on the shoulder. "I'm going to surrender to Lysent. Get that bounty."

Had they all gone crazy?

"Audra promised she'd take you there if you turn."

"And you believe that? She's not going to take me. She's never given up on anyone."

That wasn't true.

Dwyn hadn't known Belinda. Audra wasn't really open to talking about it — or anything really, for that matter — but he knew the two had been on their own for the longest time. The Audra he knew now had emerged from that relationship's tangled roots.

Gordon opened his canteen, which steamed with citrus and bitter pine. He tipped the mouth of the container toward Dwyn. "Besides, it's not if – it's when. I have a fever."

Dwyn felt his heart drop lower in his chest. It just wasn't fair. Gordon's health was deteriorating. Lysent's stance was that Gordon deserved it for not having the financial means to go through 'proper' channels, that Dwyn was safe because he was well-connected. But neither of those things was in Dwyn's or Gordon's control.

What was in Gordon's control was a decision to trade his body in for food and fuel for his family. And soon, he would lose that opportunity as well.

Dwyn gave a nod and a flick of his eyes for Gordon to join him. They topped off their canteens with more tea before heading toward the rail line and its easy navigation to Lysent corporate headquarters.

*   *   *

After having navigated to the grocery store, Audra appreciated her half broken-in trails. She opened her gait and coursed through the woods. Endless pines, oaks and sweetgums crowded the trail, giving Audra a bit of camouflage as she pushed toward the highway.

I-16.

She and Dwyn had left several in cars along the highway. They would be easy to check on, gather, and bring home. The rest were spread out. They would take time.

Audra had time.

This was something she could do. She couldn't cure the z-virus. She couldn't medically tend to the sick. But she could round them up before bounty hunters did. She could keep them safe until the world could be made safer.

The chill in the air kept her body temperature down, allowing her another level of speed impossible to sustain in Georgia summers. Dwyn had wanted to come, but he never would've kept this pace for the hours Audra would. His top speed was always faster, but she had the endurance to run for what seemed like forever.

Audra's breath caught in her chest, not from her exertion, but from thinking about Dwyn. It wasn't lost on her that she had sent him to speak with his ex-fiancée after assuring him the woman still had feelings for him. Dwyn's feelings for Audra were earnest, but she had pushed him away so many times. A relationship would demand Audra communicate emotions and vulnerabilities. It was easier to stay closed off. It was easier to run. She just wasn't sure how easy it would be to watch him move on.

Hours passed before Audra popped out of the forest and onto the highway. Large swaths of wire grass had died and fallen. Their brown streaks matched the rust of the decaying cars, shoved and overturned by Jack's old convoy. That convoy was sorely missed now. If they had managed to hold onto those vehicles, they could've gotten the hell out of Dodge, leaving Greenly and her wrath behind. Or, even she could've just gone and escaped the punishment of watching her mistakes snowball into another outbreak.

No matter as it was all wishful thinking. Without vehicles and a reliable source of fuel, they were locked in.

It didn't appear any vehicles had come through since the convoy. No bustling cars. No terror here. She raced down the highway on foot, pine straw and empty plastic bottles crunching underneath her feet. Despite the throes of winter, human touch was being eaten away by vegetation, streams, and trees. The median and the other side of the highway were indistinguishable from one another. Their phase on Earth might be snuffed out before it ever got started again, the remainder of them just a second round of fertilizer for a new, peaceful world.

Audra ran until things almost looked familiar. She slowed to a walk, peeking into shattered windshields and warped windows. With the highway changing and yet the same mile after mile, it became one thing to remember she'd left a young girl in a sedan and entirely a different thing to remember which sedan. Audra's mind began playing tricks on her. Had she missed her or was she gone? The attack she suffered on this highway clouded and crowded her memories.

Just as Audra convinced herself she needed to backtrack, she caught sight of the cherry red, now rusty red, vehicle parked at an odd angle on the shoulder of the road. The antenna had been bent into a zig zag at the top. Her mark. Approaching the rear passenger door, she wiped the filth off the window with her sleeve to get a better look. Her heart dropped to her stomach.

The little girl was no more.

The door handle gave with a creak. The familiar odor was not overpowering, just a part of her world. The body slumped against the opposite window and door. She pulled the decaying body down until it was lying on the seat cushion. Her skin had mottled with green and gray hues.

Audra walked around and opened the opposite door, ignoring the bodily fragments left behind. She forced the girl's eyelids over the emptiness. Audra pulled the yellow tag off the brown ear — a tag she had left when she abandoned this girl. She wiped the flesh off the tag against the back of the passenger seat before putting it in her pocket. Her breath stuck in her throat.

As she climbed out of the car, she looked around for something to leave her. No flowers to be seen. Just winter and death. Audra walked through the drainage ditch and into the forest, climbing a tree to cut down some boughs of evergreen. The somber woman folded and braided, scratching up her arms with the sharp needles and protective bark, until she had a half wreath for the girl. She crawled back inside with the bones and sinew to wrap the head in a green offering.

Audra gently shut the door. She turned around and she finally broke, her knees buckling, her back scraping the crustiness on the door. She let fat tears roll through her hands to her knees underneath.

Audra had found that girl alive, and instead of helping her, she had checked to see if she could use her for gain. When she couldn't, she trapped her without any way to get food. Lysent said they would round them up and keep them safe. Lysent lied. And Audra knew Lysent lied. She had left her there to starve and rot.

It seemed those were the only options left — starve or rot — but in trapping that girl, she was no better than Lysent.

Wiping the tear-filled grime off her hands, Audra pulled out the list of names bountied, really sentenced to death, because their paths had crossed Audra's. A heavy burden of grief settled over her as she realized she had knocked out half of this list herself. Many to ash in the trailer she had traded Greenly. Lysent needn't even bother. She was doing fine killing them all on her own. And their faulty cure — that would do the rest.

Despite the barrage of death, Audra climbed from the ditch where she sat. If this tag was untouched, then there was a chance the others on the highway were also undisturbed. She tightened the straps on her bag, and marched on, determined to help at least one person on the list. Her list of failures.

CHAPTER EIGHT
TAGGING

Audra braced herself with a deep, heaving breath before she approached the black car. Her stomach twisted in knots. Would the teenage boy she and Dwyn left in there be dead? Gone? Audra hoped for the latter over the visual confirmation that another had died.

She muttered a little prayer as she used her sleeve, nasty from the red sedan and her breakdown, to clear the window. The black-brown muck didn't allow itself to be removed as much as it simply shifted to the sides. Audra fell back in surprise as a mass charged at the window. Teeth snarled atop receding gums. They smacked the glass with a clunk. Gray orbs for eyes bulged. Audra's ass hit the asphalt and she laughed in surprise before more closely examining her captured tag. He had already sunk back in his seat, having depleted the energy available to him. The teenager's papery skin had a sheen of grease. His stomach and lower legs bloated and no fat or muscles to speak of, but he was alive.

Audra poured water through the partially opened

window, noticing rain stains along the interior of the door. Carcasses of a few rodents lay on the floorboard. Rats seeking rotting flesh to find it wasn't quite dead had sustained the teenager — Link Culpepper as the bounty list had reminded her. Link lapped up the water, his swollen tongue scraping along the filmy surface of the window.

Pushing into the woods, Audra searched until she found a small rodent den. Building her snare with sticks and a wire, she baited it then repeated the process at another den. She wished her traps luck. Hopefully she'd catch a mouse. Even better, two. One for Link and one for herself. Hedging her bets, she foraged before setting up her tent within visual range of Link's vehicle. She wanted the opportunity to protect him if another tagger came by.

Soon she had a rat for her pal Link. She bled it, letting the rich liquid flow down the window for his consumption. She then fed him bits at regular intervals late into the afternoon. Link revived with a new energy. The virus was a curse and a blessing for the resilient human body. She yanked the rusty door open and Link fell out. Getting to his feet, he followed her just as he had when she first met him. However, walking was slow. His feet dragged and twisted underneath swollen ankles. Audra forewent the leather mask. Link deserved the full experience of a change in scenery.

When she approached her next stop along the highway, she tied him to a yellowing side view mirror a few cars away. She knew what she'd find. She braided another bough of pine greenery before approaching the car. She laid it gently around the elderly lady's bones. She picked the tag off the seat where it had fallen and put it in her pocket with the others. At least no one else would try to make money off of her body.

Audra had done enough of that.

Monetizing the sick. Monetizing the dead. She and everyone else had survived only to betray the last of humanity. They deserved whatever was coming. A second outbreak. A wiping out. An extinction. They had failed spectacularly.

Audra distracted herself by searching the ground as she led ambling Link. Lars and Lindon would have covered these miles after attacking her and stealing her pack. Besides being hungry for a few days, Audra had lost several personal mementos. While she knew chances were slim, her eyes swept the road and her feet kicked over loose debris. A carved figurine. A discarded photograph with Belinda's smile. Seen just one more time. Audra yearned for a reminder, but not for the person. Belinda would be out of her mind with terror if she had to face the looming threat of reversion. Where Belinda was, fear could no longer wrap its claws around her.

Better than a physical memento, that was something to hold onto.

The tautness and angle of the leash changed ever so slightly behind her. Only years of pulling zombies allowed her to sense the change, even if she couldn't explain it. Link looked straight ahead, but not at her. Beyond her. Audra's eyes followed but saw nothing. She pulled him off the highway in any case. He sensed something she didn't.

A pack of men tromped down the road past her and Link's hiding spot. Eight men she didn't recognize. Either travelers or just venturing from the safety of Lysent townships. Were they hunting tags? Hunting her? If so, they'd continue on the highway where they'd find boughs decorating dead bodies. She hoped they'd let them rest.

Audra decided to continue on not using the roads. Link would move even more slowly, but they'd move more safely.

*　　*　　*

The residents of the motel tensed as Audra entered with Link. The few tables were filled with people, playing cards or eating. Always eating. Ryder stood over a pot of steaming stew. Audra hoped there was at least one group out foraging for food to replace what they'd eaten today.

"Another one?" a man with deep ocher skin and slick black hair said around the food in his mouth.

"Yes… I'm bringing him here because it's quarantine," Audra said slowly as if they were kindergarteners forgetting yesterday's lesson.

Ryder stood back, not supporting Audra's idea of quarantine or pointing out the man's hypocrisy.

"I just don't see the point. We have no doctor. No cure. Just this dusty motel to die in," he said, having swallowed his food.

Audra felt heat rising over her collarbone and creeping up her neck. She covered half the distance to the table. Link pulled ahead on his leash, limiting her movement.

"I didn't clear out this entire place for you to die here," she answered with a cold calmness.

"No, I think when we turn, you'll go back to Osprey Point. This is just your dumping ground," started another person at the table. "And we don't want them here."

Audra launched forward, grabbing Link by the back of the shirt before barreling toward the table and stopping just short. The Snow White derivative — jet black hair, unnaturally white skin, and lips splattered with rat blood — did his part by pulling and snarling. Link acted like Audra felt.

"What the hell!" came shouts, which just riled Link further as the complainers tumbled off the bench, trying to find distance. From the corner of her eye, Audra saw Ryder rushing over. She didn't have much time before the situation would be yanked from her hands.

"While he looks like a monster to you, this boy's name is Link Culpepper. His family was evacuating the coast when he succumbed to his illness. We will keep him safe until a cure can be found. And when you get sick, we will do the same for you. Even though I don't like you as much as I like Link."

Audra pulled Link away from the table. She heard Marcos stifle a giggle from the corner. Ryder stopped short of intervening, shock on her face. The people stood up and brushed themselves off.

"This isn't a dumping ground. You're welcome to leave if you don't like how we do things." She waited for the woman who called it such to make eye contact with her. "But you should know. Lysent is hunting those who have lived outside their system — you. You will not be treated well if you fall into their hands."

"Why? We didn't do anything wrong."

"Apparently they believe in us more than we believe in ourselves. They see us as a threat that needs to be eliminated. So let's trust each other to outlast this bad break and see each other through — turned or not."

"Where will you keep him?" asked Ryder, hesitating

and mousy. "We don't have any more spare rooms."

"In mine," she answered.

"Where will you stay? Surely not in there with them."

"I'm not staying," she said plainly as she escorted Link to her room.

"She sure does like the young boys it seems," giggled someone from another table.

Audra ignored him.

With Link deposited into her room, Audra immediately turned about face and began to head out.

"If anything happens to Link or Kip, I'll make sure the same happens to you," threatened Audra. There were nods all around. Apparently she had gotten through to some, or at least scared the heck out of them.

Ryder walked with her to the gate. "I know you want to help them, but aren't there more important things to do?" she asked softly so the others wouldn't hear.

Audra reeled around, "There is nothing more important! I won't sit back and let my tags be scooped up for slaughter. I won't."

At one time Ryder felt a duty to the sick and vulnerable. Now she argued for safety. What did safety matter if they lost their humanity for it? She let the gate bang open in the crisp air and didn't stop to close it.

They were good at that.

CHAPTER NINE
SISTERS

Dwyn and Gordon decided to meet up with the rail line and follow it to Choros, the township housing Lysent corporate headquarters. While it wasn't the most direct route, it was the least complicated. Not having the years of Audra's experience in traipsing through the woods, they didn't want to chance getting lost before completing their tasks.

They gave Uno a wide berth when they neared it. As a township that had sent out taggers, they couldn't be trusted. If anyone recognized Gordon, he could be detained and sent to Lysent. And while that's where Gordon wanted to end up, he didn't want anyone besides his family benefiting. Dwyn promised he'd trade the credits for food and fuel and deliver it to Haleigh.

For the first hour of walking, both men were wrapped in their own thoughts. But Dwyn realized he'd work himself into a frenzy worrying about all the worst-case scenarios of his current venture. He imagined Gordon felt the same in his contemplation.

Dwyn decided an effort toward small talk was necessary, if only to keep out of their own heads. Gordon must have had the same idea.

"So, you were a tagger when you met Audra?" he asked abruptly.

Dwyn laughed. "Audra wouldn't say so. I was uh, pretty green."

Dwyn remembered his fumbling attempts to scan zombies before Audra had taught him the ropes.

He recounted his job placement. "After they woke me up, they explained to me that during the outbreaks, many people were 'misplaced' in the chaos. Taggers reunited the sick with the healthy. It was a crock, but I was required to have employment and 'Lysent goon' didn't have a lot of appeal."

"You think this bounty is a crock?" asked Gordon. His face flushed with either the exertion of the hike or with his illness. Dwyn himself felt a little warm.

"You'll get something, but nothing worth your life."

It was Gordon's turn to laugh. "I'm not sure my life is worth much. I wasn't there for Haleigh and Eliza at the onset. I was in that damn laboratory, and what did I accomplish? Nothing. And now, I can sit in my room and revert, or I can give them something."

Dwyn hated it but it was Gordon's decision. And it wasn't even a horrible one. He was sacrificing himself for his family. A decision many had made over the years. Audra tagging for her sister. Vesna's fatal push to dampen Lysent's rule. Ziv to cure the half zoms. And maybe Corette. What was his sacrifice? And whom was it for?

"Is it weird going to see your ex?" asked Gordon, pulling Dwyn from his reverie.

"Well, yeah. Audra could just be talking shit because she thinks this is the best play. Corette could hate me. Turn me in for a few bucks."

"What was she like before? Hell, what were you like before?"

Dwyn realized he hadn't really discussed it with Gordon. Their past lives were so different, they didn't really seem relevant. But then again, maybe he hadn't changed much.

Dwyn blinked and instantly could smell her lavender perfume. "She was a dancer and I was head over heels. I couldn't believe she agreed to marry me. We were so young." He paused. "After all this, I thought maybe I had loved her more than she had loved me."

"Young and idealistic. Me too — I thought by staying in the lab, I was going to save the world."

"Will you hang back until I feel things out at Lysent? I mean, uh, how sick are you?"

"Low-grade fever still, but it's just a matter of time, right? Lisa has already reverted and I was before her. But yes, I can try."

"A low-grade fever? Dude, you got time. What if we took a little detour after I meet Corette?"

"Detour? We'd already be there."

"I'm just thinking, you could go up and see your little girl. I'll watch out for you, make sure you get where you need to be. Keep everyone safe. I am after all, a tagger."

"You'd do that for me? Don't you need to get back and… save the world?" Gordon looked at him in earnest.

"I'm saving my part," he assured Gordon. "Plus, if I can buy some time, maybe I can convince you not to sign yourself over to the corporation."

"I'm not sitting around."

"I know, I know," Dwyn assured him.

But those weren't the only two options.

Dwyn raised his arm and ran his fingers along the silver links of the fence. He could almost make out the melody. A small song in the woods. Dwyn thought of Corette's sweeping lines and wondered if she still danced.

*　　*　　*

Dwyn showed Gordon a spot by the creek outside the Choros fences. When Audra had business in Choros, she was often here instead. He smiled as he remembered Audra running off with his clothes when he was bathing there one day. She and Vesna had really taken him under their wings. They introduced him to this new world and showed him that it wasn't that bad. Only the people who lived in it and made it bad were the ones that soured it. And Vesna explained that could be fixed. They could eventually overthrow Greenly and Lysent. And he, in turn, had convinced Audra. But did it all start here with Corette? Was she the first one in his life to take a stand against Lysent's principles, so that he could do the same?

Even though he hadn't made a name for himself as a tagger, rebel, or anything in between, he still felt nervous standing at the gate. Tall, bulky guards stood in front of the massive timber block gate. They had upgraded since he was last here.

The two men, almost identical in size and color, said nothing to him. One waved his hand, a signal to someone hidden. And mechanical noises accompanied the opening of the gate. Dwyn cautiously stepped inside, but no one stopped him. It seemed Choros had become so confident that they were open to public business.

Dwyn took a deep breath, fighting against his shoulders arching into his ears. He wasn't sure if it was being so close to Lysent headquarters or the possibility of seeing Corette that was making his entire body tense. He stiff-marched up the main drag, which had been dressed in cobblestone. It seemed that being close to headquarters had its perks.

No one paid the man any attention as he entered the gated plaza, rounded the fountain, and walked up the tall white building's steps. The tall windows glistened and when Dwyn entered the marbled lobby, he thought the combination magnified the light. No matter the weather outside, it was just brighter in the Lysent building.

A mahogany desk sat center, like a sentinel protecting the administrative keep. A woman with round cheeks and dark hair that fell in coils sat behind it, her fingers deftly separating paper from file. Her brown eyes matching her desk looked over their papers to see him standing there.

"Dwyn!" she said, taking no time to recall his name. "How is she?"

He knew whom she spoke of. While she remembered Dwyn's name, it was Audra who held a special place in Rosie's heart.

"She's doing well. We're all doing well. Thanks to you," he said with a somber smile.

Rosie had saved Belinda from being slaughtered with a simple paperwork error. And she'd saved the entire laboratory by warning them about an incoming attack.

Rosie gave a soft smile as if these things were basic duties in her line of work. Then the smile turned mischievous and her eyes sparkled.

"Are you two…?" she asked.

"No ma'am."

Rosie shook her head. Her soft curls echoed the movement. "It's not good for a person to grow up alone out there like she did."

"She had her sister," reminded Dwyn. Audra could make connections. Belinda was proof.

"She had a burden," Rosie corrected unapologetically. She straightened a thick stack of papers, and then immediately placed a larger, more disordered stack of papers on top. "So what can I help you with, tagger Dwyn?"

"I was hoping you could connect me with someone."

"Isn't that the job of a tagger?" she asked, amused.

Dwyn smiled. If he was still tagging, the fact he hadn't seen Rosie in the last year did not bode well.

"Corette Ku—" her maiden name of Kuzma trying to roll off his tongue. "Corette Godin. She awakened me. I'd like to say thank you."

Rosie squinted thoughtfully. "I do think it's time." Dwyn wasn't sure what that meant, but at least Rosie seemed willing to help. Rosie straightened in her chair as if returning to her administrative duty. "I will arrange a meeting for you, at the creek, outside the fences, tomorrow morning."

"Thank you, Rosie."

"No problem, dear. Don't give up on Audra, all right? She's been through more than most."

Dwyn nodded, already anxious to see his Corette.

*   *   *

Audra ran. More, she sprinted until she was out of sight of the motel and even the highway. Sooner than she was ready, her lungs began to burn and her legs slowed without her permission. Sweat stuck inside her shirt, pulling her skin. The space between her nose and lips moistened.

Her tags would die, just like those in the semi-trailer, the open roof billowing with smoke, ash, and flame. She pumped her arms ever harder to get the last of her sprint until her feet stumbled. Her face careened into the pine needles, scraping the high of her cheeks and neck.

She lay there for just a moment. The silence. The constant silence. Just her heavy panting into the dirt, the heaviness of her pack, and nothing moving within earshot.

All dead.

She snapped off her bag and rolled over. Dark branches scratched through the overcast. Dead leaves. Dying earth.

When her breath settled in her stomach and slowed, she pulled herself up against a small poplar. Pulling out the list once more, she tried to ignore the names of those already lost. At least others would be searching for bodies gone. Instead, she racked her brain to remember all the tags she had left in secure locations, locations where they'd have been able to survive.

Audra used the poplar tree to pull herself up. She needed to hurry. Time would kill anything Audra couldn't reach.

Hours of running led her to back roads that slipped

through overgrown fields. Green tractors, sweeping arches of irrigation systems, hay balers and their decaying rolls scattered along the farm land. These places supported the food supply for thousands when thousands was just a drop in the bucket.

It wasn't good tagging grounds though. It seemed those who fed people didn't get much in return. Most families from this area couldn't afford to awaken their loved ones. By the time the awakening process was set up, farmers had already shared all their knowledge and skill to help others survive. They had nothing left to trade.

A fallen sign for Hunt Drive signaled to Audra to turn from the asphalt road to a gravel road. She peeled the sign from its tangled nest and chucked it into the field. The ground was evidently disturbed, but at least undeniable confirmation of the spot had been removed.

Audra traversed the lengths of a couple of fields before she reached the head gate on Hunt Drive. A metal sign hung a good ten feet over her head. Hunt Farm. No way she'd be chucking that sign. She walked underneath the graying archway.

The large two-story house had probably looked imposing before, but now that the exterior was falling apart, it seemed even more intimidating. Its sunken wrap-around porch, jagged like teeth. Shutters falling off hinges as sagging facial features. Audra tiptoed on the floor joists of the porch. An open front door allowed anything to come and go, animals and spirits alike, but also offered rain water and vermin to any occupants within.

Kaci and Sofi Hunt were high school-aged daughters of the Hunt Farm apparently abandoned when they turned. Audra wasn't sure what would push the Hunt parents to leave such an advantageous spot, but then, she had also never lost offspring to a gruesome disease. A storm must have passed through to leave the exterior in such disaster. The interior was otherwise intact.

Audra stepped into the foyer and waited. She hadn't made much noise, but for hosts that hardly ever had visitors, it would be enough. Moisture from the elements had crept into the space. Where tile protected the floor, shoes lined against the wall rotted underneath damp fallen jackets. The hooks on the wall remained stalwart, but the walls were stained and pitted.

Audra was surprised no one had come to greet her. She looked up the stairs, following the wrought iron rail up to the second floor and its balcony hall. Past the stairs were several doorways. A large kitchen with an island bar, breakfast nook, and butcher table. A dining room with the furniture perfectly aligned — never used before or after. Audra entered the open living area with a double fireplace, dried-up throw pillows, and intact couches. And sleeping bags. And camping supplies.

Audra finally heard someone approach, but it wasn't decaying twins coming with a pitcher of lemonade and neighborhood gossip. It was boots on the porch joists and the rattle of a door unsticking from the tile on the floor.

Shit.

Audra stepped softly but quickly into the back end of the kitchen, out of view of the foyer. Opening a door, she found the laundry room as well as Sofi and Kaci. Their buttery blond hair crept down to their waists, blending with their pearly skin with a jaundice tinge. They had the same sharp noses and even tilts of the head as they turned to look at Audra. Audra left the door open a crack. She might need a diversion.

She heard cackling laughter bouncing in the foyer as she slipped into the walk-in pantry. The door creaked open but closed with a dry click. She hoped the twins hadn't caught sight of her entering her hiding place.

"What was that?" Audra heard a thump of two bodies and the laughter ended.

Audra was left in the dark. She hadn't even seen the entire interior of the pantry before she closed herself inside. Afraid to shift her feet, she pulled out her dagger and bent her knees, ready to strike if someone opened the door.

They were silent and she was silent. Then Audra heard the rasp of labored breathing as the women migrated across the kitchen.

"Oh hell, the twins figured out doors," a deep voice announced. Heavy boots met the women's barefoot steps and ushered them back into the laundry room. A scraping sound as something was braced against the laundry door. The back wall of the pantry backed into the living room and Audra could hear two other people – which matched the number of blanket piles Audra had seen.

"That'll keep 'em," the voice gruffed in the kitchen.

It would keep more than just them. Audra's eyes adjusted to the light coming through the bottom of the door and saw the pantry floor clear. She allowed herself to shift her feet.

She'd be here awhile.

"Wanna try to fish?" asked a voice in the living room. "It's been warmer these last couple of nights."

"Yeah, yeah," came a voice which shifted with the owner's movement through the house.

"I don't know why anyone'd leave this place," laughed someone else, matching the grating laugh that had first traveled through the front door.

"Well we're gonna have to, to take these girls to Lysent. I'm thinking we stop by Osprey Point on our way there. Maybe we can grab someone else."

The three rummaged around and bantered for a bit before she heard them pass through the kitchen for the back door. Audra recalled a pond out back. Laughter was right. This would have been a wonderful place to bring Belinda. A modern home where she could pretend the world was normal minus the Internet and cable television.

Audra gave the men time to settle in their fishing spots. She didn't want someone retrieving something they'd forgotten while she was out of her hiding spot. With the house continuing its silence, Audra opened the pantry door. It gave with a low-volume, but high-pitched complaint.

Audra paused again to assess for sounds that were not her own before she slipped out into the kitchen. Tall windows and a windowed patio door looked out to the pond a hundred feet away from the house. Audra decided they'd have trouble discerning motion inside with the glare and refraction.

As Audra tried the doorknob of the laundry room to verify it hadn't been locked, the chair placed against the door slid then clattered to the floor. Audra didn't see any reaction from the men outside. Inside, the girls faced each other and rocked from foot to foot in sync with each other. Audra had never seen such behavior. Had they inadvertently hypnotized each other? Audra didn't have time to think about it. She wrapped her silk cloth around the wrist of each, attached a lead, and walked them out of the kitchen and into the foyer.

After navigating the broken porch and crossing underneath the Hunt Farm sign, Audra helped them pick into a run. With good form (for zombies) and coordination to stay upright, the girls could have been track stars. They left laughter and fishing in their dust... although Audra did laugh herself as she thought about the men trying to understand how the girls had mastered the barricaded door and escaped.

CHAPTER TEN
CONNECTIONS

He waited. He didn't know if she would come. He hoped she would come, even if it was just to tell him to leave her alone. Then he'd know. But he wouldn't know if she didn't come. If she didn't come then maybe she was too scared, or was stopped, or didn't trust. God, he wasn't making any sense.

Dwyn watched the water flow over the river stones. The bright blue sky reflected in the water, making it appear clearer than it was. After long runs, he and Audra would soak their feet in the cool water, rubbing their blisters and hot spots on the smooth river rocks, massaging sore muscles. It was one of the rewards of running — the pure relaxation that could follow. He wished he could reach that place now, but instead his stomach twisted in knots and his heart danced around, even though he commanded that it slow. He was here to ask for her help in upending a corporation, not for her hand in marriage.

He remembered when that had happened too. He had taken her to a fancy dinner. She loved to dress up and eat a three-course meal with white tablecloths and where the server placed the napkin in your lap. Dwyn always found the places rather impersonal, but he liked to watch her there. She could be so sophisticated with her sly smile. Dwyn didn't even remember dessert. They had two options, and he didn't remember which one he had. He was too nervous. He paid for dinner. He must have, else they wouldn't have let them leave, right? And now they were walking down the sidewalk. He gave her his jacket. She said she didn't want it. It was quite warm.

Oh, so it was.

"Can we walk through the park before we leave? I really like this park."

"It's a little dark," she remarked.

Was it?

"That's OK – let's just go to the fountain. It's lit up. I want to make a wish." He smiled broadly.

She smiled back. "OK."

She didn't complain that he was making her walk in her nice heels. Later they'd realized the leather on the back of one was ruined after getting stuck in a crack between two concrete insets. And when they got to the fountain, it was beautiful. The prism of colors from the lights flashed and made the fountain look much prettier than it actually was. They had spent many an hour here, making wishes, and spending time with each other.

He kissed the penny and tossed it in, but instead of making a wish to the fountain, he knelt down in front of Corette and held out a velvet box with a ring.

"Will you?" he asked.

"I will," she said.

And his wish came true.

Or, no it actually didn't. He had forgotten that for a second. His wish had not come true. Months later instead of leafing through their wedding planning book, they were running for their lives. It was a different hand in hand. It was a nightmare.

"Is it you?" someone asked of his back.

He was sure he was doing something, but he wouldn't remember what later. He turned and saw her. She looked just as beautiful as when they had first met, although she had matured much more. Dwyn was behind a few years for all his slowed metabolism. She hadn't had that experience, instead she had experienced much more. Subtle wrinkles accentuated her dark eyes. Her thin nose leading down to lips and perfect teeth were just as he remembered, but her dark brown hair was sprinkled with fine gray. She had worried, struggled, and fought to survive. And she had. She had even carried Dwyn through to this new place and world. She was the reason he was there. And he was so thankful.

"It is. I… I… thank you," was all he could muster as the tears flowed.

"What?" she approached him cautiously.

"Thank you for curing me. I have all of this because of you."

"It's not much. I'm sorry I couldn't give you more," she said with a concerned smile.

"It's so much. I have a chance out here."

"May I give you a hug?" she asked.

Corette walked toward Dwyn. Her steps were so graceful. Long legs creating perfect lines.

Wrapping his arms around her, he found himself wrapped in that familiar lavender scent.

He couldn't help himself. It burst from him before

he knew it. "Do you love me?"

"It's not that simple."

"I know that. Boy, do I know that. But, I just need to know what happened between us."

"Nothing happened between us. It happened to us. You got bit. I had to survive on my own. I found someone else."

The last sentence stung Dwyn.

"Do you love him?" he asked.

"I couldn't find it in myself to kill you after you turned. But I mourned you as if you were dead. Eventually I met Hiram. And yes, I do love him."

Dwyn let go and nodded his understanding. He was thankful for what he had, but it turned out, that was all he had.

"I'm so sorry about Vesna." It was her turn to burst out.

"What do you know about Vesna?" he asked, confused.

"I knew her. She recruited me, same as you later. I swear I didn't know what Greenly had planned."

Dwyn's head was spinning. "Wait, you're part of the rebel network?"

Corette nodded, her light skin paled.

Dwyn's face broke into a giant grin. At the same time, his eyes teared up.

"How many of you are there? In Lysent?"

"Just a handful, but we've all worked to key positions. I work in the armory. Clyde has access to the entire campus."

"Your husband, Hiram?" Dwyn tried out his name.

Corette shook her head. Dwyn didn't push.

"Do you know if the corporate cure is still working?"

"No, I don't know. I've tried to find out. Something is definitely going on, but they're keeping it under wraps."

Dwyn wasn't sure if the non-answer was better than confirmation he was at risk for reversion.

"Do you know what she has planned?"

"I know she's gathering her forces. Training the zombie soldiers. I think she's going to war, but I don't know who against."

Dwyn smirked. "Probably us."

Corette's eyes went wide. She hugged him tightly.

*   *   *

Satomi jumped in surprise with the whine of the lab's door. She thankfully landed back on her stool, not falling to the chilly floor.

Satomi finger-combed her hair and hoped Marla hadn't noticed she was sleeping. She couldn't sleep at night, and she couldn't stay awake during the day. The only consistency was her inability to get anything done.

"Sorry to bother you," said Marla.

Marla didn't appear to have sleep problems. Her eyes shined brightly underneath her dark spectacles. Her wavy red hair was pulled into a fluffy ponytail.

"What is it?" Satomi rubbed the warm spot on her forehead, which was probably red and wrinkled from its pressure on the counter.

"There's… there's someone at the gate."

Satomi's eyes went wide. She could hear the worry in Marla's voice now. What was Satomi supposed to do about someone at the gate? Audra and Ryder, their capable leaders in war and peace, had left. Satomi was more apt to hide than to answer the call of a stranger.

Crap. What was she going to do?

"Is Jack around?"

"He was out gathering. I don't know when he'll be back."

There wasn't much she could do besides climb the scaffolding and speak for Osprey Point. Satomi somberly stood up and pressed the wrinkles from her long lab coat before taking small steps to meet Marla at the door.

Several people were already outside with melee weapons, waiting for some signal to attack or scatter. Across from the fountain and atop the scaffolding, Satomi saw the brunet and blond pair of Branson and Tess, arrows nocked. Satomi couldn't recall ever climbing up there.

She gripped the rough pine sides and worked her way up, trying not to rock the structure. She trusted Ryder's engineering skills, but heights were another matter. Positioning herself between Branson and Tess, Satomi put her hand on the edge of the solid metal barricade positioned on the fence. It rattled, echoing in the forest. Pulling her shaking hand back to herself, she peered over the fencing.

Three men stood below. A long-faced man with blond dreads kept two horses. A large man with a wiry red beard kept Jack, blue knit hat askew and his arms bound behind his back. He looked up at Satomi with an apologetic grimace.

The redhead cried out a greeting. "Hallo good scientist!"

Satomi blinked. She didn't recognize them, but apparently he knew who she was. Or maybe it was just the lab coat.

"Hello. What uh, can I do for you? Why do you

have my…" it was hard to say it, "friend?"

"Well, he was out here all by his lonesome! Haven't you all ever heard of the buddy system?"

"Of course, we just don't have a lot of hands to go around," she said before realizing her mistake.

Tess snickered next to her. Jack hung his head. Satomi wondered again why they had no one better to stand up here. She should not be up here.

"Well, that's a shame," said the man with the two brown mares. "We're here for your turn-backs."

"Turn-backs?"

"Ex zombies, gonna-turn-agains, I don't care what you call them. Whoever's sick or is gonna get sick again," he explained impatiently.

"We don't have any of those," said Jack, helping Satomi. "They hit the road. Didn't want to be here when they… y'know." Jack shrugged his shoulders to accompany the end of his sentence.

The redhead's voice grew raucous. "Hey, I'm getting them off your hands. They're going to turn any day now and you're going to be behind the walls with them, running for your life. I'm just making this easier. Taking them to headquarters where they can get treatment and safety."

"Are they also going to get some cotton candy and a pony?" asked Jack from the corner of his mouth, but loud enough for Satomi to hear.

The broad man tugged on the bindings, throwing off Jack's balance in response. Satomi didn't need Jack's comment to know their proposal wasn't favorable. They were rounding up the sick for Lysent, but why?

"Look, you can either let us in, or I'm going to kill Blondie here." He used his leverage to rock Jack by his bindings once more.

Jack looked up and met her eyes. A few weeks ago, Satomi would not have been bothered by such a threat. It was not lost on her that Jack was now in the same position he had forced her into just months ago. His family had brought a great amount of fear into her life. But, she could not wish the same for him.

"Please, don't," was all she could manage.

"OK, then we'll just come in."

Satomi heard an electronic beep before a clap of noise. Metal plating and chain link flashed in her peripheral as the east side of the fence was tossed and scattered. The scaffolding swayed. Marla and several others lay on the ground, stunned.

"Now we've got one more of those planted along your place," said the same but distant voice. "Bring out your dead — soon-dead I guess — and we'll be on our way without destroying another thing."

Satomi's vision blurred with panic. Everything seemed to be tumbling down. "I'm telling you!" she screamed. "WE DON'T HAVE ANY HERE!"

The man shouted back, ragged and angered. "Then we'll take YOU, Peter Junior here, Peter Senior, and Audra! You guys are worth more than turn-backs anyway. I'm tired of talking shit with you."

Satomi wasn't sure where it came from, but a sick laugh erupted from her mouth. "You think if Audra was here, that you'd be talking to me?"

Hot stingers of tears collected in the corners of her eyes. Why did Lysent value her life? How was she a threat? She understood that Greenly must've run Evelyn's DNA and figured out who the family was — creators of the army she had confiscated. And Audra was a big pain in their butt, but why Satomi? And why turn-backs? If Satomi's antiviral was the only faulty version, why not just let Osprey Point revert and die off?

Maybe she had missed something.

And maybe it was too late. Maybe Peter's creations were about to march in and cut them down.

What was she going to do?

*   *   *

Heading to warn Osprey Point of marauding taggers, Audra wasn't far when she heard the explosion. She considered dropping the sisters' leash to reach the community faster, but if they were taggers, the sisters would be of high value. Instead, she pulled out her knife and reached back, making a shallow slice into the back of her shoulder. She felt warm liquid trickle into the small of her back.

Now they were moving. The sisters became frenetic. The growls and snapping kept pace behind her as they raced down the road toward Osprey Point. Three men and two horses stood at the gate, and they turned to address the tiny stampede careening toward them.

"Oh, ho ho, Blue. There she is!" The man with curly red hair laughed.

Audra pulled to a stop, but the zoms, having spotted and smelled the sweaty horses, continued forward. Audra set her feet and held on like an owner with eager dogs.

"Oh, and she's got some for us," said Blue. His cowboy hat hid his dark beady eyes.

Audra recognized them both. Manny and Blue, two of Greenly's zombie shepherds.

"They aren't for you," countered Audra. "Haven't you killed enough of them?"

Audra had escorted them to her trailer of sick and they had set it aflame. The next day after the fire had burned out and the metal had cooled, Audra dropped down into the chalky remains, breathing in the ash, helping the last of them pass.

"Now, we do regret that. Mostly cause now they're worth money."

Jack's eyes were wide at the sight of Audra's pets. Manny kept an arm around him. A large knife swung from his belt.

"Everyone OK in there?" she asked of Satomi, who was perched atop the fence.

"Um, they blew up part of our fence. Say they got another one ready if we don't surrender some people."

"Did you tell them you didn't have any tags?" she asked as she wrestled with the leash. The horses whinnied and stomped worriedly.

"Yes, told them all the reverting left so we wouldn't be in danger. But now they want me, Jack there, you… Jack's dad."

"And those," the shepherd reminded her again.

"These are mine. I've tagged them — now more than once. Finder's rights, you know?"

Audra's anger settled as flames flirting with her collarbone. It wouldn't be the first time she had to defend her tags.

"Well, then I guess that makes Peter Junior here ours," laughed Manny. "You're out there tagging again?"

Audra didn't answer, which gave him his answer.

"Then maybe we can strike a deal. You give me the duo and I'll leave you guys alone for a bit. I'll even hand over Jack here. He can help you tag. When I return, you hand over more valuable zoms or that scientist. I don't really care which. Call it rent, protection, whatever."

Blue smiled at the proposal.

Audra thought it over for a moment. "These two for Jack?" she asked to clarify.

"Sure. For now."

"And what if I don't?"

"We set off the other explosion and take everything."

Manny and Blue both cocked their heads to wait on the answer to their offer.

Audra's pair continued to pull toward the large sources of meat as if they were eager to go. It would be easy to hand the girls over. Arguably, Jack and the others inside were worth more than the forgotten Hunt sisters. Osprey Point's inhabitants had lives to live. This duo didn't.

And yet, she couldn't push the burning trailer from her mind. Those lives lost were on her. And so would these be.

It wasn't worth it. Her heart — her soul — couldn't take another death.

"Take me instead."

CHAPTER ELEVEN
TRADE

"I know there's a bounty on my head. Am I worth more than these two?" she asked.

"Quite a bit," said Manny, nodding. He appeared to think it was a good deal.

She was sure it was. If Lysent had decided that she was this important, then maybe she'd make good on their evaluations. She heard murmurs of disagreement above her.

"Audra, you don't have to do this," said Jack. "We can fight them."

"There's no need." She wasn't going to let the shepherds have any more of her people. She wasn't going to let Lysent dictate what happened here. "It's time to end this."

"Audra, stop. I'll go," pleaded Jack. His eyes were wide with surprise.

Greenly having the half-zom army's controller. That was the last thing she needed.

She ignored him. "You'll let my zoms go into Osprey Point." She couldn't very well lead them to the motel and the jackpot of tags who lived there. "And I'll come with you."

Manny untied Jack and pushed him toward the biting zombies. "Take 'em," he grunted.

"What the hell's going on?" asked Jack in a rough whisper as he took the lead from Audra. Audra tucked the folded bounty list in his front jacket pocket.

Manny placed Jack's bindings on Audra. Jack straightened his beanie and met Audra's gaze one more time. His eyes asked if he needed to make a play. Audra gave a small shake of her head. She knew he wouldn't interfere without her permission. Dwyn would have been another story.

Audra gave a nod up to Satomi, Branson, and Tess, hoping they wouldn't worry. She then departed with Manny and Blue, who had not mounted the horses. Too much distance from Audra and they'd get arrows in their backs.

After removing themselves from range, the men hopped into the saddles. Manny put his hand out for Audra. She didn't accept it. She'd rather walk. He didn't mind. He laughed.

He allowed Audra a long lead to follow behind them. Even with the space, the horses kicked up dust and grit into Audra's nose and mouth. She worked her kerchief from her neck onto her face with shoulder shrugs and neck contortions. Still, it was better than being hip to hip to these shepherds. She remembered their crude behavior. She'd keep separate from them as long as possible. The rope scratched and scraped her hands and wrists. It was nothing like the cloth ones she used for her zombies. The horses smelled of sweat and manure. Or, maybe that was the men.

With the bounty list, Audra hoped Satomi would be

able to piece together why Lysent was intent on scooping up zombies and scientists alike. They needed more time, and she was giving it to them. But that wasn't her only reason for trading herself.

Audra thought of the dead in sedans, the ash of the trailer, the angry, lost, and sick at the motel. She and Larange Greenly had something in common. Everything they touched — they ruined. Perhaps they should meet their matches.

Audra had no delusions she'd survive Greenly, but if her scorecard had anything to show, Greenly wouldn't come out of it alive, either. And that she could deal with.

Manny and Blue continued down the road, joking with each other and passing a flask back and forth. Audra assumed it wasn't water. She used to have that life. She didn't have a horse, but she had a flask and the joy of a good cash find leading up to a fine fire, good spirits, and a good night. Audra knew they wouldn't make it to Lysent headquarters before sundown at this pace. That gave her time to come up with a plan. Greenly would meet her. She was sure of it. But she'd still have her guards with her. Audra wouldn't be able to do much to Greenly.

Whatever she did, it would have to be quick. And life-changing.

Perhaps she could sneak a blade. She imagined plunging it into Greenly's carotid. What would Audra do as the woman bled out? Smile? Laugh? It'd be easy to watch someone who created such chaos be put in their place.

A slow light rain highlighted the scents on the trail. Despite the overcast, it'd be a beautiful time to run. But for now, her hair stuck to her face with the moisture. Brushing it away with her bound hands just scratched her face with rope.

After hours of walking, they reached a boarded-up gas station. While the weeds, scattered vehicles, and debris made the place look abandoned, the fact that all the windows and doors were closed and secured, was a sure sign that someone was using it. The bright reds and blues of the brand had faded to oranges and grays. Manny and Blue dismounted and began walking the horses to the back. There they found a ratty wooden fence, but a fence nonetheless. It slanted and swayed. Several boards were missing or broken. But the gate worked, sort of. Manny pulled up on it to get it to move. They led the horses in and tied them up. The wire grass inside had been flattened — the horses had been here before.

Blue lifted his shallow chin toward the back door. The metal handle had been knocked off the heavy door. Audra looked at him expectantly, but did not move to go inside. She wasn't going to go in first or second. Hell, she wouldn't even go in at all if she could help it. In there, she'd be trapped.

"Get in, girl," pushed Manny, his growl devolved into a thick cough.

She cut her eyes at him, trying to size him up. He was still large and grizzly. More than she could handle. She remembered what he had told her when they first met. She'd better watch herself.

She might never see Greenly.

He opened the door and Blue pushed her in. So much for holding her ground.

For its boarded windows and front door, the inside was still not as dark as she had expected. A large hole in the one-story ceiling was to thank for that. Audra looked at the floor where the hole made a spotlight. She saw the markings of past fires underneath, old coolers on their side around it to sit on. Against the windows, shelves stood as a secondary barricade, much like at Haleigh's community. Prepackaged food items were long gone, but their discarded wrappers littered the ground, gathering dust and decomposing even more slowly than their dying consumers.

In the corner, blankets sat. Their beds. Audra didn't want to investigate them any further. Besides the obvious, the bedding seemed to be crawling with thin roach-like bugs.

"If I agree to get on the horse, we could make it to headquarters before it gets dark," suggested Audra.

"Nice try. It's gonna get dark fast. And 'sides, we don't need to go just yet," Manny added suggestively.

Audra didn't have any preconceived notions she'd be treated well. It didn't matter as long as she had enough strength to kill Greenly in the end. If it saved the reverted, made a difference, even better.

"Don't scare the girl, Manny," said Blue. Then to Audra, "We know what you did to those shepherds, but your payout at Lysent is worth much more than getting revenge for the two SOBs that couldn't survive a little girl." He smirked.

Audra wasn't sure if that was true or if there was a bit of respect there.

"Then why don't we go to Lysent?"

"Cause their listed bounty for you is shit!" he laughed.

Negotiation. Audra understood. She sighed. She didn't have time for these petty greedy transactions. She needed to get to Greenly and end it. At this point, if she'd had any credits to her name, she'd pay them to deliver her to Greenly. Preferably with a weapon in hand. But she in fact had a very large debt in the Lysent system. It hadn't seemed to matter much, until now.

"I'll head out in the morning and talk to 'em," said Blue. "Manny will stay here with you."

Manny wiggled his eyebrows.

Audra flopped her butt onto the ground and let the two build a fire for them.

*   *   *

Satomi volunteered to help in the repair of the fence at Osprey Point. Marla nervously pulled on her shirt's hem as she directed people. It was her first project without Ryder and she had her work cut out for her. The explosive wasn't just a scare tactic. It had taken out support beams and Osprey Point didn't have much in the way of supplies. This side of their home would be weaker for many months to come.

"We can add a set of cars on the exterior. They can help support the fencing for now, but I'd like to cut trees and perform the repair sooner rather than later," Marla said, scratching her head between waves of curls and looking down at her half-scribbled plans.

Satomi helped dig out the remainder of the telephone posts that hadn't been blasted away. Another shovel contributed to her work with Jack sidling up to her.

"Hey, I'm sorry I got caught like that."

Satomi shook her head. She dived her shovel's point into the hard dirt. "That's why we don't go out alone," she lectured.

The potential to be grabbed or held hostage wasn't

the only reason to not go out alone, but in this moment she allowed it to be so.

"Thank you for not letting them kill me," he said and smiled.

"I didn't do anything," she said. Anger directed toward herself and a particular dirt clod. She wasn't quite sure what to do with the thoughts churning in her head.

"No, no," said Jack, dropping his shoulder and put his hands lightly on her arms. "You kept them talking. You kept them from killing me. You had a choice. You could have taken one look at the situation, laughed, and gone back into your laboratory. You don't need me. You don't like me. I did… awful things." He let his arms drop.

Satomi tied her hair up into a ponytail with the elastic from some old clothes, giving herself time to think. As much as she wanted to hate Jack and punish him — she couldn't.

"I couldn't let them kill you. You're not a bad man," she admitted more to herself than him.

Jack had made horrible mistakes, but since his sister's death, he busied himself caring for his father, defending the community, and working harder than many of Osprey Point's original inhabitants. Satomi considered the mistakes she had made. She wasn't 'bad' either.

Jack gave a nod and started back digging.

"After this, I'll go out and search for Audra." He sighed. "We lost her."

Satomi gave a small smile. "I doubt that woman's out just yet. She's either got a plan in mind or she's at least giving us an opportunity."

While Satomi had beaten herself up for mistakes

still unknown to her, Lysent didn't seem to hold the same mindset. They didn't want her working. And if that was the case, then that's exactly what she should be doing.

Jack wiped the sweat from his brow. "Opportunity for what?"

"To do what Lysent doesn't want us to do. Cure your father."

*　　*　　*

After helping with the fence, Satomi stepped into her laboratory. It felt like an entirely new place. She was thankful to be there, to have a chance to work. And with her decision made, she no longer felt lost.

Satomi pulled open a drawer and removed the notebook she had kept under her shirt when Audra came to negotiate her release from Jack and Jill. It contained the protocol for creating a peptide that might not only bring Peter back, but would also be the first beneficial application of the z-virus. Satomi opened the refrigerator to confirm the medium for building the peptide remained untouched. It might have been useful in working on the antiviral. Instead, it would be helping the father of the virus.

Jack coughed at the door to not surprise her. She jumped anyway.

"Sorry," he said.

She gave him a look and he apologized for his apology. She had asked that he stop apologizing so much. She was ready to move forward.

"I'm going to escort Audra's zombies to the motel," he announced. "Is there any message you want me to deliver to Ryder or anyone else?"

Satomi's eyes moistened at the thought of getting a message to Ryder. She'd be pleased to know Satomi was working toward something to help them. She only hoped her friends still thought she was capable. She ripped a sheet from the back of the notebook and began trying out the pens for ink.

"God, Dwyn's going to be super pissed, isn't he?" asked Jack. "She disappeared on my watch."

He rubbed the back of his neck.

"She didn't disappear. She chose to go. But yeah, he's going to be upset," she said, not looking up from the start of her letter.

"Maybe we can form a search team, try to find her, try to back her up. Whatever it is she's doing."

Satomi had learned a long time ago Audra never asked for permission or advice before running headlong into things. Satomi wasn't the same.

"I'm glad you came in, I need your express permission to treat your father." She paused. "I don't think he's lucid enough to understand and give consent. I will be injecting the z-virus into his body, which we currently don't have a cure for. This treatment is highly experimental. It could kill him, maim him, or otherwise infect your father."

Jack thought for a moment. He gazed at the beakers on the counter, the lopsided microscope on the table. Jack never thought they had a cure to begin with.

"My father was a risktaker. If there was a chance he could become whole again and useful, he'd do it in a heartbeat."

Satomi couldn't help but ask.

"Was your father… a bad man?"

Jack huffed at the question, leaning on the back of a stool. "I don't really know how to answer that. He's my dad. I never thought of him as a bad man. He worked at his job. He did what he was told. When things started going to shit, he knew exactly what it was. Shit they were working on. He did what he could to protect us. Always. And so did Evelyn and I after that. I don't think we're good people — not like you guys. We're just... surviving. I think my father would help with the cure if he could. It drove him crazy that he couldn't figure it out on his own. I think he'd help you."

Peter was a pleasant man now, but that did not mean he'd remain that way. He could become less than cooperative, combative, with his intelligence back. That wouldn't be her fault though. Peter had done wrong, but it wasn't Satomi's place to judge him. Only Lysent held back treatment based on agendas and selfish protocol. Satomi would no longer do the same.

She finished her letter to Ryder and started pulling supplies off the shelves to take the treatment from paper to injectable serum. It was time to take action.

CHAPTER TWELVE
RECONCILIATION

Dwyn picked up a long, straight stick along the path. Its bark stripped, it had already done time as a hiking companion before it had been discarded. Dwyn used it to provide support as he climbed root systems that wove over the surface of the hill like a waterfall. The steepness required some amount of focus, so he was allowed to not speak to his partner constantly.

Instead, Dwyn tried to wrap his mind around a world in which his ex-girlfriend plotted for a corporate downfall and secretly recruited him. There had been some amount of deception in bringing in Audra. He was naive to think that it wasn't the same for him. She could also be lying. Pretending to be on the inside to get information from Dwyn.

But then, why wouldn't she lie about loving her husband? Why be honest about that, when it could turn him away?

As if waiting until they crested the hill, Gordon asked, "What if they hate me?"

"Audra said they loved your note. They're going to

love you all the more," encouraged Dwyn as he considered dropping the walking stick. It could help someone else down.

Dwyn looked behind and saw Gordon slowing down.

"I don't know if I deserve to see them."

Gordon stopped.

Dwyn backtracked to him. It was obvious something was bothering Gordon. Dwyn nodded toward a couple of fallen logs and swung his pack off. Gordon did the same, plopping down on one of the logs.

"Haleigh didn't tell me she was pregnant with Eliza until after the divorce was finalized. She said she wanted me to decide on her as a wife, not as the mother of our child."

"Whoa, that's rough, dude," was all that Dwyn could get out.

"I was too focused on my career. I got the job at Osprey Point shortly after we got married. I was publishing papers. Working with our largest client, Lysent Corporation. I didn't put time into our relationship.

I was angry when I learned what she had kept from me, but more so I was embarrassed. It had seemed easier to let her go than to change my ways. I figured what was the harm."

Gordon kicked at a rock, which rolled over. Tears streamed from his eyes.

He sighed. "It's taken pandemics, world restructuring, and a god awful long time for me to realize what really matters. I should have fought. I should have fought before the divorce. After the divorce."

"And now," recommended Dwyn.

"And now. So even if they hate me… because they have every right to… I'm still going to go and fight for them, for us."

Dwyn placed his hand on Gordon's shoulder. People's problems weren't erased by the z-virus. In fact, at times they seemed highlighted by it.

"Ready to go fight?" Dwyn asked with a grin.

Gordon wiggled back into his pack.

"We're not far. That was the last big hill," Gordon stated as he kicked the gray rock off to the side of the trail.

Dwyn leaned his stick against the logs for someone else or perhaps his future self.

It wasn't far at all to the tiny town. Dwyn couldn't imagine a giant grocery store here. It must have landed here after someone in corporate fed data into an algorithm, no one actually bothering to scout out the site.

"It's down this way. Across from the bank," Gordon said, picking up the pace.

Dwyn started in a trot to follow him. As they turned a corner, the store came into sight. By the road, a couple hundred grocery carts lay scattered and tossed.

Dwyn guessed the carts were not where they were supposed to be. It sent Gordon into a frenzy. He ran headlong into the mass of carts, hopping, tripping, and climbing. Dwyn followed more carefully. He noticed some carts were tied together when they fell. They created odd pyramids and ramps over cars.

Gordon cleared the carts and leapfrogged over them, yelling Haleigh's name all the way through the parking lot.

Gordon pushed his way into the store and disappeared into its depths. No one stood atop the store. Inside, trash, supplies, and debris lay scattered on the ground. Blood. No one in sight.

It didn't bode well. Dwyn pulled out his knife and waited at the door.

Deep guttural sobs started from the produce section of the store, moving through the aisles. It seemed to shake the entire core of the store.

There wasn't enough blood on the floors. And there were no bodies. The carts had been trashed.

Where was everyone?

What had happened here?

*   *   *

Audra's shoulders ached. Besides breaks for the bathroom and a single meal, both her wrists and ankles remained secured. And yet, Audra refused to ask for reprieve. She didn't want to owe Manny anything and she didn't want to be touched any more than what was necessary. She just needed to survive the next few days. Then, she'd be delivered to Greenly.

Two nights passed at the gas station before Blue sauntered in and slid onto a moldy cooler.

"Sup?" asked Manny, tossing Blue a bottle of water.

Both Audra and Manny were anxious to know the results of his negotiation. Audra for its time frame. Manny for its monetary value. Blue spat tobacco onto the chipped linoleum floor, shaking his head and a few days' worth of scraggly facial hair.

"She's drawing it out, Mann. Doesn't want to pay up." He kicked a stone into the fire. Sparks flew and died.

"She don't care about money. Why she stalling?"

"I been thinking. Maybe she doesn't need her, just needs her out of the picture."

"Out of what picture? Osprey Point?" Audra couldn't help but ask.

"Sure, she wants your whole crew," said Blue. "But they don't seem so difficult to round up, especially with you out and the group split between there and the motel."

Greenly knew about the motel? Audra felt adrenaline building in her body as she realized she had left both locations vulnerable.

"Take me to Greenly," she demanded. She needed to finish this.

Blue raised his eyebrows. "Why you so eager to die?"

"You promised you'd take me to Greenly! I'm going to kill her."

Audra fought against her wrist bindings. Her shoulders burned in protest, but the rope-made creases had gone from numb to raw. At Osprey Point, she felt useless. Here, she felt like a ticking time bomb.

Both men watched her and laughed. Manny finished with a hacking fit.

"You doin' all right, Mann?" asked Blue, passing the bottle of water back to Manny.

"I'm fine," he grunted, wiping spittle from his beard before taking a sip from the bottle.

"For now," his friend mumbled.

Audra paused from her temper tantrum.

"You were cured?" she asked.

"Apparently not," said Manny, his voice dripping with bitterness.

She'd have known if they had cured him with their

faulty antidotes. They hadn't.

"What do you mean?" she dared to ask the giant man. She needed confirmation.

"Turn-backs. Folks everywhere turning back."

Jack was right. It wasn't just their stock; all the antidotes were bad.

"Does everyone know?"

"No, Lysent's covering it up — blaming you guys for having sleepers in the townships…"

By blaming Osprey Point, none of the townships would be taking proper precautions. Greenly wouldn't be able to keep up the lie indefinitely, but until then, Audra expected many townships to fall. All the Lysent-cured were at risk.

Dwyn.

Dwyn had been cured by Lysent.

Audra struggled to not be sick as she considered it. Dwyn's face going ashen, drool in the corners of his mouth, reaching out to her with bony fingers. Dwyn was on borrowed time.

Audra realized she was too. She was being held ransom, and just because they had shared information didn't mean they were helping her. It just meant they didn't think it would matter soon. Audra pushed the rising panic down.

Killing Greenly wouldn't fix this.

"You need to let me go."

*　　*　　*

"We have to find them," Gordon said, his voice rife with panic.

Dwyn stood frozen for a moment at the store's entrance, not sure how to say what needed to be said.

"We will," he started. "But we can't, right now."

Gordon's face contorted in anger. Dwyn considered the possibility that his friend was about to punch him out. He took a step back, but Gordon fell to his knees.

Dwyn approached to comfort him, but Gordon waved heavy arms out to maintain his space. Then, his hands went to the floor to support him as vomit spilled from his mouth.

Gordon was getting sicker.

He sat back and wiped his mouth with his dark jacket sleeve. He leaned against some boxes.

Dwyn knelt down to him. "Something went down here, but I don't think they're dead." Gordon whimpered. "They moved, or they were moved. But we're just going to have to trust Haleigh to do what she's done for years — keep herself and Eliza alive. I promise we're going to get to the bottom of this. We will find them, but for now I have to get back with my information, and you're getting worse. If you stay out here, you'll turn. Then you'll never find them, or worse, you will."

Gordon didn't move or respond.

The mess on the floor stung Dwyn's nose. He wanted to get some fresh air, but knew he couldn't leave Gordon alone.

"I'm so sorry. But let's write them a note in case they return here. You found them once. We can do it again."

He pulled Gordon up and they went to find something for a note. After what seemed like a long time, they finally made their way around the carts outside.

Gordon looked back. His eyes swept the store

front.

"How could I have run out of time?" he mumbled. But it had been a long time coming.

*   *   *

Satomi decided against bringing Peter to the laboratory for treatment. It was an unfamiliar space with familiar objects. She didn't want him to be upset or scared, nor did she want him to latch onto latent memories that might pull him in a bad direction. Who knew if that's how it worked. It was all experimental.

Instead, she prepared a tray with sets of syringes for a house, or room, call.

Jack had returned from dropping off the sisters whom Audra apparently considered of equal value to herself. He delivered Satomi's letter and notified Ryder and Marcos of Audra's latest excursion. He sat with Satomi as she worked.

"OK, I'm not reneging my consent or anything, but if I'm being honest, I don't see how infecting my father with the z-virus is going to make things better."

Jack then began to spin on his stool, so Satomi wasn't sure how serious he was in his statement.

"Well, what does the z-virus do?" she asked.

He reached out a hand onto the counter to stop his motion. "It turns you into a stupid brute that eats people. Like I said… not an improvement."

"What else does it do?" Satomi asked as she put a pot of water over her Bunsen burner to boil.

"Well, it makes you hard to kill."

Satomi nodded. "This virus is the most pervasive and the most enduring the world has ever seen. Upon infection, it replicates and hijacks the body and mind, shutting down higher thought processes and stimulating hunger in the presence of other potential hosts."

"Yeah, the feeding… You're not selling me on this." He gave himself a single rotation around as his reward.

"— the other part of its success, is that it protects the host. It boosts the brain's natural defenses and repair functions because the longer the brain stays intact, the more opportunity the virus has to spread. That's the feature we're exploiting. I'm hoping it will repair the present damage and restore your father's mental capabilities."

Satomi took the pot off the burner and poured the water into the teapot filled with pine needles she had collected this morning, and dried mint and ground dandelion root.

"Those upgrades only come after the virus replicates and reaches a tipping point in the body. The peptide I synthesized will signal to the virus it has already reached that tipping point, starting its protective processes. If we can keep a certain level of the peptide in the bloodstream, it should curb viral replication so it can't get out of hand. And if we develop a cure, we can completely eradicate the virus from your father after it's cleared out all the damaged cells."

"And the mindless cannibalism?" Jack asked.

"Hopefully not so mindless."

There was an awkward pause before Jack realized it was a joke.

"Funny. But, really."

"Really, the viral load in his body should be so low that he won't develop any of the unwanted characteristics."

Jack spun one more time, his head back. "My dad, the zombie."

Satomi arranged the treatment series on the tray and added honey to one of the tea cups.

First, Satomi infected Peter intravenously with the z-virus. No matter how Satomi rationalized it, it went against everything she had vowed when she took on the title of doctor. If her highly experimental treatment did not work, Peter's body would become infected with a virus that had no cure. He would lose the little but crucial amount of brain function he had left.

Peter was cooperative for the first injection, but when Satomi informed him that the rest of the syringes were also for him, he began to get suspicious. Jack held him down as Satomi introduced into his blood the peptide that signaled to the virus it had replicated to capacity.

The peptide was something the virus naturally produced whenever it replicated in a host. As the peptide built up in the body, it slowed viral replication, giving the virus a form of self-regulation so it wouldn't overwhelm and kill the host. By synthesizing and introducing the peptide earlier, Satomi was attempting to use the virus's own systems for the host's benefit. She only hoped it would work.

CHAPTER THIRTEEN
TRANSITIONS

The next day, Satomi didn't notice much of a difference in Peter, except that he had fewer angry outbursts. It could have been her imagination, but if not, it indicated an increase in his ability to cope. Even if that was all that came of the treatment, it had possibly improved his quality of life and hadn't turned him into a ruthless cannibal. But still, hoping for more, she and Jack said nothing to each other. They both stayed silent, as if speaking of the possibly imagined results would make them disappear.

Turned out, they could have discussed it loudly for days on end, because it was working. Satomi treated Peter with the peptide until the levels in his blood matched the levels in fully infected individuals. Short-term and long-term memory was recouped. His working vocabulary increased. He followed complex trains of thoughts and had his own.

Not all returns were pleasant. Soon, Jack and Peter were huddled together in tears over Evelyn's death. Peter pulled at his hair and mourned, really mourned, for his daughter. Peter hugged his remaining child tightly. They cried together, laughed together, and cried some more.

Satomi gave what she hoped was an appropriate amount of family time before knocking on Peter's door. She was called to come in and she quickly joined them around the wood veneer table.

Peter actually physically looked different. The hard lines in his brow and jaw had softened. His posture relaxed and his shoulders slumped. He still wore a buttoned shirt, but the collar was loose and Satomi noticed a couple of wrinkles in the shirt. Perhaps all that neatness had been an attempt to find order and peace. Satomi hoped he was now content, and wouldn't press forward with absurd experiments.

"Hi Peter, do you remember me?" she asked.

"I don't have any memories of you before my illness," he said, his eyes searching. "But I know you now. You drink tea with me." He nodded his cup to her.

"Yes, I do. I'm also a scientist and a doctor."

"I was sick, but I feel better than I have in ages. Did you give me something?"

"I did."

He jumped up from the table, his chair falling to the floor. Satomi found herself wrapped in a huge bear hug. So far, so good.

"How did we meet?" he asked, all smiles, still holding her in his arms.

"…your children kidnapped me."

A giant backhanded blow hit Jack in the jaw.

"I'm sorry, Dad. I didn't know what else to do!"

"You got your sister killed and you kidnapped this lady! Is she still captured?" he asked incredulously, looking around to verify if the room was a jail cell.

"No, no," Satomi explained. "Your son released me. I brought you both back to my community, where we're trying to fight the epidemic."

"Oh," Peter said, looking down at the ground. "That."

"Yes, that. Were you working on it too? Is that how you got sick?"

Satomi gave him a moment. Peter returned to his chair and uprighted it.

He shook his head and let out a low chuckle. "I got sick because I tried to vaccinate myself. I knew the cures weren't working and I couldn't get it to work. I figured the next best thing was to bolster our immune systems so that we wouldn't catch the damn thing."

"That didn't work," encouraged Satomi.

"No, it didn't," he confirmed.

✳   ✳   ✳

Audra pushed soot around on the ground with her boots. They were still bound, and the movement kept her feet from going numb. Despite involving her in discussions, Manny and Blue still didn't trust her.

They were giving her too much credit.

The combination of her self-initiated stagnancy while Greenly planned her strike and the poor ventilation from their indoor fires left Audra feeling dumber with each passing day. Blue had left again to negotiate payment for her head. Apparently, Manny wasn't allowed in Lysent headquarters due to his preexisting condition, which was an appropriate policy given that Manny's health was precipitously declining. The stupidity of it all made her want to scream. She stomped on the ash.

"Need to go out, little dog?"

She ignored the question. Even the dimness of the remaining evening couldn't hide the fact that Manny didn't look so good. Sweat poured from the crevices of his red face.

"Manny, you're turning. Let me help you," she said, willing her voice to remain steady.

Manny exploded in anger, shouting, "You can't help me, you stupid little girl." He grabbed a metal rack and threw it against the shelves. It made a clattering noise that echoed off the wall of refrigerators. He wiped his brow with the soaked sleeve of his jacket. "No one can."

It wasn't the first thing he had thrown that day. At least nothing had been directed toward her yet — ricochets excluded.

"That's not true. We have scientists working on it. We're taking care of the sick until we can cure them."

She needed him to see reason before reason became impossible.

"Ha! You can't pull this shit again. Lysent already fooled my folks. They're in debt up to their eyeballs for my first cure."

"…That's why you're selling me," she realized aloud.

"I want to at least pay back my worth before I turn back."

He flopped down on his bedding, sending a scurry of generic insects in multiple directions.

"Please, let me go. Neither of us has to die from this."

Audra couldn't think of a more pointless death than being eaten by Manny the Zombie. Stupid.

"That's where you're wrong, pretty. I've held you hostage for days. If I let you go, you're gonna kill me or keep me for your weird collection. This way, we're both dying from this."

"I won't take revenge," she promised. "I don't want it."

"OH HELL YOU DON'T! Why else would you offer to be delivered to Greenly?"

"I thought she was only hurting Osprey Point to get to me."

"Her plans are bigger than a grudge," laughed Manny. His red hair stuck on his head with sweat. He leaned against the browning plastered wall.

"I know that now. I need your help. I can't do it alone… no one can do it alone." She recalled Dwyn's constant reminders.

Manny hacked into his sleeve. Looked down at it. His nostrils flared with surprise and fear. Was he coughing up blood? Manny was going to turn and Audra would have to watch, arms and legs bound.

"Too bad you are alone. So am I." He slumped over and was quiet for a few minutes before he began to snore. His body heaved with the effort of his breathing, and convulsed periodically with fevered sleep.

Audra felt her eyelids grow heavy. She responded by adjusting her shoulders and sending searing pain down her back. As she listened for the snores to end and the snapping of teeth to begin, she searched the thrown debris for something to cut her binds. Eventually she settled for the sharpest rock bordering their fire circle. She finagled it behind her back and began scraping against the rope. If nothing else, it was something to do.

* * *

As the sun faded, Manny didn't stir to build their nightly fire. There wouldn't be much time before their abode was enveloped in darkness. Audra risked standing up, balancing with ankles tied. She hopped, scooted, and pivoted until she reached the door.

It was jammed up.

Audra started on the windows, pushing the shelving with her shoulder to see what, if anything, gave.

"What are you doing?" asked a voice behind her.

She turned in surprise.

"Just trying to find a way out of here before you turn and eat me," she said coolly.

"Sit down. I'm not gone just yet." His voice scratched.

She backed around him and returned to the cooler where she was sitting. The rock still hidden in her palm.

"Drop the rock."

She dropped it without a word.

He came up behind her again and this time Audra gagged from the smell of his yeasty sickness. She felt her ropes tighten then loosen. They fell to the ground. Her shoulders cried in their sockets as she brought her arms forward.

"Build a fire," he said.

Audra did as she was told, but kept a close eye on him. He was leaning up against a shelf, slouched partly over. He pulled out a flask and drank heavily from it. She figured he had been saving it all for this night. It was not a night for savoring, but a night to die. She hoped it wasn't hers too.

In leaning the logs, Audra's hand dragged across a

large splinter of wood. Risking the noise, she snapped it off as she positioned the kindling. She peeled some off the end to crudely hone the tip to sharpness. She'd only get one chance to stab something vital. She tucked the shiv into her sleeve and started the fire with one of the matches.

Matches.

What an odd thing for these shepherds to carry. Why carry matches instead of flint or another reusable fire starter? Modern conveniences must die hard.

A large belch emanated from the corner as the fire sparked up. The flask lay on its side, done. He started to bob his head up and down, the sickness and the alcohol making his eyes float in his head. Audra didn't ask about her bindings. And he didn't seem to remember them.

"Anything I can do for you?" she asked. There wasn't much that could be done. Bind his hands? Ha. Sing for him? God, she hoped not.

"Not a thing, honey. No one can do nuthin' for nobody. We're alone here. It's been a long time coming."

"I'll at least boil some water so you can have some to drink."

"Have some to throw up, you mean."

That was true too. But she imagined that the moonshine he downed would be enough to vomit for a bit.

She poured water from the bucket of unboiled into the pot. She set it up against the flames. The guys hadn't bothered to find a grate or anything to cook upon. They subsisted on barely boiled water and jerky and protein bars provided by Lysent. All of their supplies, she thought of the matches, were bought from Lysent. She bet the shepherds were kept on a pretty tight financial leash just as the taggers were.

"You put me out of a job, you know. Now she got that army, she don't give a shit about the herds I push around. Now they just rotting in the corrals. Worthless like me." He spat just inches from himself.

Audra hadn't really thought about how she had turned the system upside down. Shepherds. Taggers. Zombies. She had caused a lot of trouble, but right now, she found she just wanted to help Manny. Give him some moments of peace and keep him company. Something her sister didn't have. Audra repositioned the pot to get it into a warmer spot. She wanted it clean and cooled off for him. It was the least she could do.

It was one thing to turn once. It was another to know it was coming again.

Audra's body threw itself onto the hard floor without her permission as the explosion rang out, shaking her bones.

When the echo in her ears subsided, she could feel the coldness of tile on her cheek and the silence. The smell of copper reached her and she turned her head to peek.

There he lay flat, not far from her. A large crater formed at the top of his head. Blood and wads of soft material splattered on the floor. A sawed-off shotgun between them.

Audra stood up, her teeth rattling. The sight wasn't all that unfamiliar, but the explosion of noise and the fact that he was there — and then he wasn't — sent adrenaline coursing through her body.

He was alone.

And so was she.

A shocked, bitter laugh escaped her lips. She

couldn't convince Manny he wasn't alone any more than her friends could have convinced her. With Manny gone, she could still make her way to Lysent. She could surrender to Greenly, try to kill her, hope this madness stopped.

Or, she could stop demanding to be alone.

Audra heard the creaking of shelves and plywood.

She reached for the shotgun, but her arm jolted in large twitches. Instead, she kicked the weapon underneath a shelving unit.

God, what poor timing. She could have been gone.

"Audra?" called out Dwyn, his voice brittle and shrill. "Are you OK?"

"I'm OK!" she responded in both relief and panic.

"We heard a gunshot. Are you OK?" came Ryder's voice, clear and slow.

"Yeah," she said. She hadn't realized they were nearby.

"We're going to get you home," Dwyn said through the door, while he pulled and pushed.

Home.

Before the water started bubbling in its pot, Audra was in Dwyn's arms. As the adrenaline faded, her upper body rang out in sharp pains from her former bindings, but the steady pressure of his body brought comfort and the sure sign she was no longer alone. She breathed in his musk and tried to settle her ragged breath. Ryder searched and retrieved the shotgun, but found no extra shells on the body.

"How did you know to look for me?" Audra asked.

"Ryder found out from Jack," Dwyn whispered into her hair as he kept her in the hug. "We were looking for you."

Audra nodded into his chest. His hands were on her

back, strong and steady. She felt their strength and imagined them curling as they ripped into her spinal muscles and dug between her ribs. Audra abruptly shook out of the embrace. Dwyn took a glance at the body of her captor and began to lead her away.

"Why did he do that?" asked Dwyn. Audra shook her head. She didn't want to tell him yet.

Ryder smiled and took her by the shoulder. "Let's go home."

"Wait," said Audra.

She poured the water from the pot, extinguishing the fire. Then inside the pot, she dropped five yellow tags. She hoped when Blue redeemed them, he'd split the cash with Manny's family. They didn't deserve the hand they'd been dealt.

CHAPTER FOURTEEN
RETURNS

In the darkness of night, the trio hiked to Osprey Point. Adrenaline and the worry Blue might return kept them moving forward against passing desires of sleep. The cold fresh air and the familiar motions helped Audra shed the lingering dread from the recesses of her brain and the shock from her frame. She appreciated that Ryder and Dwyn didn't push her to talk. Conversation would be more tolerable within Osprey Point's fences and underneath the morning's rays.

In the passing time, Audra tried to compose herself and she arrived at Osprey Point all business. She marched to the blown fence to inspect it, despite the fact that darkness still encompassed them. Ryder tried to reassure her that Jack and Marla had reinforced it and nothing needed to be done before morning. Audra took the hint and dismissed her for the night.

Ryder raced off to wake Satomi from what was probably a great night's rest. Something she hadn't had for a long while. Dwyn remained at her side, near the vague form of the fence. With the flashlight pointed at the ground, she more felt his presence than saw it. His body was warm, broad, and strong.

"People will still be asleep for a bit. Now would be a good time to wash and rest up," Dwyn suggested.

Audra noticed the way he phrased it — focusing on efficiency, rather than a reminder to care for herself. She'd let him think she bought it.

She gave a nod and followed him to the sleeping quarters. Their rooms would still be vacant. Space was aplenty again there with the potential sick staying at the motel. That's where Dwyn should be.

Audra surprised herself when she followed him into his room rather than retreating to her own. If Dwyn was surprised, he didn't show it. They both took off their boots, leaving them in the hall. Dwyn reached for a bucket of stale water and a couple of rags. He let Audra clean her face, then he helped her wash the wounds of rope against skin. It was a quiet moment between them until Dwyn began his scolding.

"What were you thinking?" he asked as they sat face to face.

He blotted the wet cloth along her neck and shoulders. The water felt cool against her hot skin.

"I thought maybe I could end it by myself," she answered distantly.

"In that gas station?"

Audra laughed. "Pretty stupid, I know."

"Pretty hardheaded."

"Have you come to expect anything less from me?"

His lips smiled in return. He stopped moving the rag, and rested his arms on her shoulders. His fingers playing with loose strands of hair on the back of her damp neck.

Audra bit her lip and looked away.

"What's wrong?" he asked.

"I'm so sorry," she muttered as she untangled from him.

She walked to the other side of the room. Dizzy, she leaned against the wall, afraid otherwise she might fall. Dwyn slowly stood up and carefully approached her.

"You don't have to be sorry. You've just been through hell. And you didn't even want to be with me before. I'm just glad you're safe and you're my friend."

Audra wiped hot angry tears that pooled on her cheek bones. She pushed them into her hair, but didn't will them to stop.

"Dwyn, Manny killed himself because he was reverting."

Now Dwyn looked like he was the one that would collapse, his knees buckling. Audra rushed her arms around him, grabbing his ribcage tightly and holding him upright. He said nothing, but he did wheeze a slight bit.

"I'm so sorry," she said again, as if that lessened the blow.

Audra felt all the things she had pushed back for so long. Dwyn had been her rock even when she wasn't accepting. He had been her comfort, even when she didn't want to get close.

Dwyn coughed and Audra pulled back in surprise.

"No, you were just squeezing the air out of me," he choked.

Audra laughed through her tears.

He gave her a small smile. "It's OK. I'm not special. Loads of people are in this situation. I know the scientists will find a cure. It's just a little scary."

And a little like fate.

"I feel fine." He almost sounded convincing.

"I have to clean up again," said Audra. Her tear-streaked face felt hot and tight.

"Why? I like the proof that you care about me!" He said, wiping her cheek with rough fingers.

Audra punched his arm. Dwyn lost his balance for a moment, but pretended he didn't. He ruffled her hair, and got his hand stuck in it.

"What do you expect? I've been held hostage for days."

Dwyn removed his hand as delicately as possible. Then, they remained close. Closer than they had been in a while.

"If you kiss me now, how will I know it's not because I'm dying?"

Audra smirked. "You'll just have to figure it out."

She leaned even closer, pressing a soft open kiss into him as she pushed away her own whys and wherefores.

It felt good to be home.

*　　*　　*

Satomi pulled out of sleep and sat upright. She wasn't sure why until a rapping on her door sounded softly. It mustn't have been the first. Her eyes refused to adjust to the moonlight as she stumbled to the door. Her sleep must have been deep. She should have cured Peter a long time ago. It would have saved her all those sleepless nights.

Opening the door a crack revealed a bright smile encased in thin pink lips.

Ryder entered the room and even though she was

small, she was strong. Satomi couldn't see much for her own hair flying into her face as Ryder picked her up and spun around. For a moment Satomi floated in the air, held up by her love. Ryder tossed her gently onto the mattress pad, quickly following behind her.

"Oh, I missed you too, Ry," giggled Satomi. She was being kissed all over.

Ryder smelled of pine and sweat. Her nose, fingers, and toes were cold, but were quickly warming up. Neither woman could stop smiling. Or kissing.

Ryder tucked Satomi's hair behind her ear. "I'm sorry I left the way I did," she apologized. "They needed me… but so did you."

Satomi shook her head and let the hair fall back. "I was lost. I found my way."

"I'm glad you're back."

"We were in different places, in more ways than one, but I'm here now," Satomi confirmed. And here, they could be together.

"Well, there's much to be done," Ryder said, each word punctuated with a kiss on her skin.

Satomi giggled and sunrise came too soon.

*　　*　　*

It was late afternoon before the group collected themselves and absconded to the conference room adjacent to the laboratory. Audra shut the door and relished the temporary peace and security. She imagined it was something no one had really felt in a while. The size of Satomi's smile was only eclipsed by the tightness of her embrace.

"I'm glad you're OK. I'm glad you're back." Satomi's eyes moistened with tears.

"I'm sorry if I wasn't supposed to tell them," interjected Jack.

Audra patted him on the back. "I'm glad you did. It really wasn't going as planned," she admitted.

The crew found spots against the walls, among the boxes of papers and broken equipment. Ryder hugged onto Satomi. Dwyn patted a spot on the ground next to him. Audra rolled her eyes then tempered it with a wink before sitting down across from him, against a defunct copier. Jack sat with his father, Peter. Peter sat with legs crossed on the floor with the limberness of his son. Audra didn't pretend to understand Peter's treatment, but he carried himself like a different person. And most importantly, Audra had been assured that he now had access to all his memories concerning the z-virus and the soldiers.

The group all left space in the middle, as if the conference table still existed. Audra's thoughts flashed back to Gordon's awakening, tied to the table and coming to after years of infection. That was a different time then. They thought they were pushing toward a reborn world. But now it seemed the catalyst for that might be their extinction.

"Greenly knows about the motel. It isn't safe, just like here. The shepherds I was with thought she was organizing some sort of strike against us. And I bet it's not going to be just a herd of rotters again." She caught Dwyn's grimace out of the corner of her eye. "I mean sick," she ended dumbly.

"Did Corette know anything?" Audra asked.

"She didn't know what Greenly was planning, but she made it pretty clear that she and several others in Lysent are ready for a change in leadership."

"That could really help us. Did she know where

Greenly keeps the half zom army?" remarked Ryder.

"That doesn't matter," spoke up Peter. "They can never be used against us."

"A failsafe?" asked Ryder.

Peter nodded. "I programmed a safety word. As soon as the army arrives, I can disable them."

"What is it?" asked Audra.

"Earl Grey," Peter shared. "But since I programmed it, it will be most effective if it's relayed in my voice."

"Could they be used against Greenly?" asked Audra.

"Technically yes, but I've come to realize it was wrong of me to create them. I took away their free will, just to keep my family safe. I don't feel comfortable using them."

"Neither do I," added Satomi.

A round of nods confirmed that those who didn't choose to fight, wouldn't fight.

There was another point to discuss. Audra sighed before diving in.

"Something's wrong with all the antivirals. One of the shepherds I was with got really sick and said he was reverting. He said it's happening all over — called 'em turn-backs. I can't confirm his story though. He killed himself before he turned, but I can't see that being a ploy."

Satomi had already been told, but everyone else involuntarily looked at Dwyn. He gave a small wave.

"I'm OK for now folks, but yeah, I'm glad I've been staying at the motel."

"Could the treatment you gave Peter help those reverting?" asked Audra.

"No, the peptide is already present in Dwyn's

blood. And what's more, Lisa's reinfection seems less receptive to the peptide. It's not a cure, just maybe a preventative measure if given quickly after initial infection."

"So what else you got?"

Peter and Satomi glanced at each other, before Satomi answered. "We need the original virus."

"What do you mean, the original virus?" asked Dwyn.

Peter clasped his hands together. "For years, Lysent was experimenting with viruses of mild to moderate illness severity, high morbidity, low mortality. They'd disperse them into the population, then sell vaccines or treatments to bolster the medical sector. It made a lot of people a lot of money. Unfortunately, the z-virus mutated almost immediately upon release. It crossed the blood-brain barrier, which had... unintended consequences."

"Understatement of the apocalypse," muttered Audra.

"So the crossing of the blood-brain barrier and shutting down high brain function wasn't intentional?" asked Ryder.

Audra thought Ryder had a good joke too, but eventually realized she wasn't being sarcastic.

"Goodness, no. It was just supposed to be a flu-like virus. When it did that and kept the hunger response active. Wow, I didn't think a virus could really evolve to spread like that."

"Why not? It's pretty effective," replied Satomi.

"Why not, indeed," he repeated.

"So, if the virus mutated, why do you need the original?" asked Audra, ready to get to the point.

"They never modified the antiviral. They just rolled

out the stockpile they had. Unmodified, it does a pretty decent job of clearing out the virus, but it doesn't cross the blood-brain barrier like the virus does. As such, the virus sat dormant in the brain and then, I assume it's mutated enough to become resistant to the antiviral. Lysent sold these treatments as a bandage for a much bigger problem."

Audra stared at Peter, refusing to repeat her question.

Satomi intervened. "Peter and I think if we have the original virus and can follow its mutations, we'd have a better shot at making the correct modifications to the antiviral."

"But there's no place that has the original virus, right? Everyone's been infected with the mutated stuff," Jack said.

"Lysent would have it," said Peter. "We had it, but I didn't think to grab any of it before we left DC. Why would we? I thought the virus was already abundant. But they had both, virus and treatment. They had to disseminate it, before they cured it."

"Do you think Lysent would have held onto it?" asked Audra.

Ryder nodded. "Yeah, they hold onto everything."

"If they have any idea of its value, I'd say yes," agreed Peter.

Satomi looked to Audra. "We need that original virus. Otherwise, we'll continue to lose this war."

"And what about Greenly?" asked Jack. "Do you think she's really going to attack?"

"We'll be ready for them," said Ryder.

"Actually, I think we'll bring this fight to Lysent," announced Audra.

CHAPTER FIFTEEN
REGROUP

Katie met Audra at the gate of the motel parking lot. 'Defeated' was the first word that popped into Audra's head. Katie's hair hung limply, unwashed. Bags hung underneath her eyes. But the fixed look of pain was the worst.

"There's no one at the gas station?" asked Audra. If Greenly knew of their occupancy here, they couldn't slack off on watch duty.

"We don't have enough people."

Audra's eyes swept the parking lot. There was no one else around.

"How many have turned?"

"Twelve and most of us have fevers. I didn't think it would be prudent to have someone outside the fences."

"Do you have enough food?"

"We have plenty of food," Katie answered flatly.

Audra thought she heard thunder following behind the rain beginning to fall. But it was the sick in their motel rooms, crashing into things, damaging their bodies, and falling back into decay. A prison of slow death. It felt strange to come here to recruit. These people were sick. But, of course, if they didn't win this fight, then they'd remain sick forever. These people had the most to lose.

"Whoever is healthy enough and willing, we're marching on Lysent."

"I will go… for Lisa," she volunteered. "Marcos and Sara will want to come as well."

"Gordon?"

Katie shook her head.

Audra walked softly up the stairs, hoping not to disturb too many trying to get rest or wandering restlessly. She stood in front of Room 13. The noises sounded distant and she dared open the door.

Audra's eyes adjusted to the darkness of the room. She saw the TV broken on the ground, and his bucket of water upturned giving the place a damp smell not unlike the rainy environment outside.

The groan discordant and husky preceded the large looming figure. Gordon's rectangular face looked wooden, like Frankenstein's monster. Besides spots of glistening drool and sweat, his skin was a flat grayed khaki.

He shifted weight on straight legs as he walked toward her. As if he knew Audra was supposed to accompany him to Lysent headquarters.

"I'm sorry, dude. It's not going to happen."

He grunted, and kicked the TV as he made his way across.

"I'm going to find your family. We're going to cure you."

Gordon's mouth more fell open than he made any

effort to work his jaw. A small cry scratched its way out of his throat. He was in pain. Audra had denied it for so long, pulling along her sister as if all was all right.

"I'm sorry. Just hang on," she whispered as she shut the door on him.

The door vibrated with a THUNK.

Audra fought the temptation to slide down against the door and cry. Instead, she climbed back down the stairs.

"When do we leave?" asked Katie. She had changed out her shirt.

"Not just yet. Get some rest. I need to take someone home."

*   *   *

His dark hair might have thinned a bit and his coloring dulled, but Kip still appeared to be an (otherwise) energetic, healthy young man. After pulling him from her motel room, she escorted him at a slow pace, so he wouldn't damage his extremities.

While this boy had been out to hurt Audra and her friends, in the end he was just a kid. Kids needed family. They shouldn't — no one should — go it alone. Winter hadn't been mild, and Audra was sure his family thought the worst.

Audra couldn't feel the tip of her nose by the time Uno's gate came into view. She approached cautiously. Audra wasn't sure if she'd be considered friend or foe. Back in the day, they had been friendly enough when she brought mail. She often brought them news others wouldn't bother to take so far, seeing as they were the farthest from Choros and Lysent headquarters. But this wasn't 'back in the day' and at least one tagger had originated from their fences.

"You got a sick?" called out the guard from atop the gate.

"I do, but he's one of yours. I've seen him around here. His name's Kip, right?"

The guard squinted to see. "Eh, let me get Moe."

"Tell him it's Audra."

Moe's rounded belly preceded his round face as he opened the gates and ushered her in a few minutes later.

"Well I'll be damned. You're still alive. Why you never come around anymore?"

Moe had kept on as mayor and bootlegger of Uno for years. They knew each other well. He looked more spherical than ever. A short scraggly thing patched on his red face. He couldn't nurture a beard like he could a bottle.

"I quit the good stuff… and Lysent," she replied. "Is this one yours?" She pointed to her friend.

"Shit, Kip."

"Yes, it seems that he got bit out in the woods."

"You don't say?" said Moe, eyeing her.

"I didn't set it up. I found him like this, but I do know what he was up to."

Moe sighed, "Now, now, he wasn't out on official township business. I don't condone his actions. But a few of our young men took the opportunity. Winter's cold. They were hoping to get food and fuel for their families."

"At the expense of others," said Audra.

"Well, that's why we're short in the first place," he said. "At the expense of others."

"Lysent takes much more than it gives," said Audra.

"And the townships too," he said.

"What do you mean?"

"We're the last on the rail line. The rations go through every township before ours. You can imagine that some take more than they should — until we're left with the scraps. Lysent refuses to start down here, work their way up, even just once a month. Greenly favors the first towns. They're closer to her. Do stuff for her, I guess. We get the short end and always will."

Another way Greenly set the towns against each other and kept them separated. It made it difficult for the townships to band together and demand fair treatment.

Audra tested the waters. "What if Lysent was convinced to turn itself around?"

It was his turn to ask. "What do you mean?"

"Greenly is blaming my scientists for the reversion—"

"Reversion?"

"Cured no longer being cured?" she tried.

"Oh, the turn-backs. We don't got any cured here. No one could afford it."

"All the cured are susceptible. Her lies and unfair policies are going to kill us. We're marching on Lysent headquarters to overthrow Greenly. It's our only chance to use the company resources to develop a permanent cure and distribute it."

"That's ambitious. We're just trying to last the winter," Moe admitted.

"Us too, but I think this is the only way we do. Would you guys be willing to fight? How about the other townships farther out like you?"

"Well, there is still the rebel network. We're a big part of it here. Some in other towns too."

Audra nodded. She had intense feelings of mistrust after Vesna's membership in this mysterious network hadn't saved her from being executed. She didn't know Corette or many of the others who claimed to contribute. But unfortunately, suspicions didn't supplant Audra's need for more hands and weapons.

"Greenly refuses to admit her cure doesn't work. She's going to sit back while our friends revert and we have outbreaks all over again."

Moe looked at Kip. He shook his head. "I don't want my kids running around trying to care for their families. We should be getting rations for our contributions. Cures should have been free a long time ago. If you're going to fight, we're in, but you know she has an army now. Some sort of robot soldiers."

Audra would have laughed at the description, if she hadn't been the reason Lysent had that army.

"Yes. They're some sort of hybrid. But, we may have a way to disable them."

"May?" asked Moe, raising his eyebrows.

"There's an 'off command', but they've been under Lysent's control for months now. Who knows if they've managed to reprogram them."

"So they are robots… What are they like?"

"They're as coordinated and agile as humans, but must be killed like zoms. Their skulls are hard, so you have to get soft spots, eyeballs, ear canal, temples, even the nose. The back of the neck starting at the base of the skull and coming up through the spinal canal—"

"I know how to kill a zom," he interrupted.

"Yeah, besides soft access to the brain, you could also bash their heads in if you have enough force," Audra added, fighting the temptation to demonstrate on Moe's round one.

Two boys ran from the center of town, rushing Audra and Moe. Both had dark hair like Kip. They took hold of his lead, keeping him at arm's length.

"Did you bring him back?" asked the taller of the boys.

"Yes, he shouldn't have been out by himself."

The shorter one kicked the taller one. "We knew he'd do it with or without us. We shoulda gone."

"Maybe, but now you're here and healthy," responded Audra. "You can take care of him."

"Until what?" scoffed the taller one. "There's no cure."

Audra dug her shoe into the dirt. "I'm trying to fix that."

The boys shook their heads unconvinced and walked off with their brother.

Audra hoped they wouldn't kill him. Although, with the pain the infected felt and no cure in sight, what was the best thing to do? She thought of Gordon recounting the wicked flames that wrapped around his bones. Maybe it was more merciful to let the infected die, but Audra couldn't let go of the possibility of healing and life.

"Let's go talk," said Moe. "Over a drink?"

"Talk, yes. I have a few questions about this train…"

CHAPTER SIXTEEN
UNO

Back at Osprey Point, Dwyn hugged Audra tightly, his face buried in her hair. She took a moment to rest and enjoy the quiet peace before saying another goodbye.

"Be careful," she finally said. "We need the network, but I don't trust them."

Dwyn was going ahead of their gathered forces to organize Corette and her people. A two-pronged attack.

"They're against Greenly. What else do you need?" asked Dwyn.

"It's just, I don't get it. They've spent years benefiting from the system. Why do they want to help us?"

"They're dealing with the broken antiviral. Same as us," he reminded her, pulling up her chin with his hand. Audra thought his hand felt warm.

Dwyn gave a little cough.

"It's OK!" he said. "Just a tickle in my throat."

Audra nodded, ashamed that she was looking for signs.

Dwyn coughed again.

Audra's heart sank a little lower.

Their goodbye was interrupted as reinforcements from the motel arrived. Six. Six people. Audra wondered if the six people could even make up in fighting power what they had lost in morale seeing just six return to Osprey Point. Tears were matched with questions and answers. Katie told them Lisa was holding up. She just needed a cure. Bradley was confined to a room without furniture as she kept injuring herself. Gordon down. And so many more friends and family.

*　　*　　*

The next morning, when Audra and her group arrived at the gates of Uno, she saw the guards there had doubled. They looked professional, much more than her own, despite their similarities. Both Osprey Point and Uno had zombies to deal with. They had to hunt and gather outside safe boundaries. They all-around had to survive a harder life than Lysent's more favored counterparts. But Uno looked much more prepared. Perhaps because those at Osprey Point were comebacks, relatively new to the world again. Or perhaps because Audra had mistakenly kept them hidden and safe.

The gates opened and her thirty or so flooded into the township, some for the first time. Audra directed them to a small building up against the platform for the train. The track looked modern and sleek, much unlike the world they lived in, even in the townships.

Moe pulled her to the side. "I thought you'd have more people."

I thought you'd be skinnier with less rations. "A lot of us have turned."

"Should've brought them too."

Audra sighed. She never saw eye to eye with the townships. There was no point arguing now.

"We have more waiting at Lysent. Tell me again about the train," she requested. She was used to hearing Dwyn repeat reports and strategies over and over. It no longer felt right to do differently.

Moe gave her a patronizing look. "Always one guy at the helm. Fifteen unmarked cars. Each with a guard and randomized cargo. I wonder whose fault that is…" he trailed off.

Guards in every car. Audra had prompted that policy when she stole antivirals off the automated and unmanned train.

Hijacking the train would give them transportation and the element of surprise. They'd be able to roll right into Choros, picking up anyone they wanted on the way. They'd arrive at Lysent's doorstep — together and ready to fight.

Would Lysent roll over or would they battle their own people? Audra knew the Choros residents would side with whoever promised them safety and security at the end. They wouldn't fight. Instead they'd wait with their heads in the sand.

"When does the train get here?" asked Audra. She already knew, but she was beginning to feel nervous. She wanted to be out of sight when it came barreling into the train station.

"3:30 Lysent time. The cold things are no longer cold. In the summer, the meat goes bad. Greens are withered."

"And these are the people that are usually here?"

Audra motioned to the men on the deck.

"Yes, some of our strongest men help us unload the boxes. Makes for a quicker transport trip. Works well for us, huh?" said Moe.

Audra nodded. She could almost feel the ground vibrate or maybe hear the hum emanating from the tracks. Whatever it was, it set her hairs on end. Audra looked at the clock which hung from an A-frame. It was early — not by much. She squinted down the tracks until it appeared into view. Audra gave Moe a big slap on the arm, unable to reach his shoulder, before she stepped off of the platform. She'd be back soon enough.

Inside the buildings were teeming with people ready to board the trains. They quieted as the silver bullet of a train swept into the station. It slowed to a stop and with a gentle high-tech bing they could hear nowhere else, all the doors to the cars opened on both sides.

Moe's front line pulled back. They had expected boxes and guards. Instead the cars were packed to the brim with people. They all wore potato burlap sacks and smelled of sewage.

Half zoms.

Shit.

Two barreled out of their car and were on Moe before Audra could consider a strategy. He was on the ground with a mouth over his neck. The blood squirted at an inconceivable height even with Moe's most likely high blood pressure. The second repeatedly stabbed him in the stomach, guts coursing. The other half zoms emerged more slowly out of the train, but Uno's first line had frozen, taken aback by the screaming and crimson of the rotund man.

"Jack, Peter, come now! Half zoms!" Audra

shouted into the crowd.

Lysent knew. Someone had betrayed them. The coup could end before it even got started. Audra pulled out her dagger — it seemed small when regarded next to these soldiers. There was no way. She looked for a melee weapon and saw Jack and Peter moving through the crowd. Jack gave her a quick nod and escorted his father toward the station.

"Earl Grey!" Peter shouted as soon as he faced his army.

The soldiers continued forward.

"EARL GREY!" he tried again, squaring his shoulders to air confidence with his command.

Nothing.

Jack tried. Why wasn't it working?

Peter ran up to a bulky man. He yelled into his face. The man only grabbed him back. Audra felt sick. Jack raced over and ripped his father from his fanged creation.

"I'm so sorry!" Peter yelled out as Jack fireman-carried him away.

Audra had known it was a long shot. The soldiers had been reset somehow. Leave it to Greenly to brainwash the brainwashed. Now they were left with only one option.

Kill.

Audra yelled out directions concerning soft spots as people finally began to rush out with weapons drawn. She ran toward the front cab which had the driver's compartment but found she couldn't ignore the half zoms consuming Moe. They pulled at greasy flesh, drawing out the feast. Audra knew others would falter at the sight. She raised her bat and swung down with all her might. It gave a mighty crack before the half zom collapsed over him.

Moe shook with eyes wide, but most of his body was gone. The second zom stood over him and brandished his knife against his smile. Audra didn't give him a chance. She knocked the smile off with her bat, his face contorting and his jaw dislodging. She raised her bat again.

"Herro?" he called out, much to Audra's surprise. Was that a hello? He shook his head as if to cast off the stars floating in his vision.

She didn't have time to decide. She swung. This time higher than his jaw. She knocked him down and swung and swung. He emitted sounds of pain, human pain. He was crying out. And Audra felt herself begin to sob as well.

He was human. He wasn't human a moment ago, but he was in this moment, this moment of death. Audra had knocked the sense into him only for him to experience being clubbed to death in some unknown place by some unknown woman. An electrifying shiver shook through her. She thought she was going to be sick. But she couldn't. There was no time. She looked up to see people fighting the half zoms, some successfully, some less than successfully. Blood sprays and screams seemed to meld together on the train's stage.

Audra pushed toward the cab. There was no way Lysent had planned to give them this train, filled with half zoms or not. She needed to stop the train from returning to Lysent without any of them on board. If that happened all of this — all of this death — would be for nothing. She reached the cab and its closed door, the only closed door. Inside, the conductor messed around with the keys and buttons on the control stand. Audra guessed he was more familiar with herding zoms by horse than driving trains. Otherwise he'd have cleared out already.

Testing the bat against the window did nothing but alert the conductor, bounce back, and threaten to knock her out. Audra had enough sense to not try again. Instead she searched the exterior of the cab. Ahead, people fought on the tracks. Safety protocols wouldn't allow the train to move with obstructions on the track. Audra had taken advantage of that protocol during her first heist.

There had to be a way to manually open the doors in case of emergency. Underneath, she didn't see any levers or any eye-catching red or yellow. Getting up, she saw some of the fighting had moved away from the tracks. She didn't have much time.

On the back of the cab, several panels were inlaid, but Audra couldn't reach. She stepped onto the connection between the two vehicles. The train jolted and Audra's body fell into the back of the front car. She put her hands up to regain her balance. The train was trying to make its getaway. It lurched, and then stopped again.

Her hand fell near a bright red lever. While she couldn't tell what it was, she imagined it wouldn't help the train go on its way. Audra braced herself with her foot and pulled. It crept down with a deep grinding noise. She heard the beautiful high-tech beep and then a gentle swoosh. She had done it.

When Audra stepped inside, the man hadn't figured out he wasn't the one who had opened the doors. He frantically re-pushed the buttons he had just pushed. He looked much larger when Audra stood in the car with him. Maybe she should have called for backup.

When he realized Audra had joined him, he searched the console again. This time Audra figured for a weapon.

With the bat in one hand, she pulled her blade from her holster and jettisoned it toward the grizzled man. She followed with her bat, covering half the distance between them. In that time, he yanked her knife from his shoulder with a primal growl. He passed the weapon to the injured arm, a small advantage.

The odds were against her. She was so much smaller. But perhaps she could keep distance or buy time with her bat. He charged at her. Audra tried to picture his round head as a baseball for her bat to meet, but she missed.

Her miss still managed to move her out of his path. He almost went straight out of the train, but he stopped himself with his hands on either side. As he shifted his momentum to bring his head and torso back inside, Audra struck the space between his shoulder blades. He only turned at the waist and wrapped one large hand around her weapon. Audra took the opportunity to wrench his injured shoulder, whipping the bat out of his hand. She pivoted on her heels and smashed it into his back.

This time he dropped to his hands and knees. She swung at his head again, again, again, until the only movement was the splashback from her bat.

A muffled static noise came from the floor of the train. A small overturned radio by the conductor's seat.

"This is Dunnbreak Township, relaying a message for Lysent Corp. You're to have departed already. Please clear the track for your return. What is your status, Blake?"

There was no telling what Blake had already told

them. In front of the train lay bodies. The train wasn't going anywhere anytime soon. Audra stomped on the radio with her boot and climbed out of the car.

Her feet had barely hit the ground when they were ripped out from underneath her.

Claws grabbed her ankles and pulled them underneath the train toward ripped lips and rotting teeth. His ears bled. Her fingernails dug into the concrete but flaked, serving as failed brakes. As her boots got close to the face, she kicked upward. Her foot freed and met his chin. His head smacked the bottom of the train and Audra hoped he saw stars. She used her free foot to stomp his face and his other hand. Prying her other foot away, she quickly backed up, hands and feet scurrying.

He did the same, backing out on the other side. Audra sprinted through the cab to the opposite door. She made short work of him with her recovered bat. Audra took a gasping breath. Her arms shook, making the bat rattle in her hands. All this death. She had just wanted to board the damn train.

Her victim's ears were crusted in old blood. Surveying the train stage, she saw he wasn't the only one.

They had emerged from the train and attacked with mouth and blade, but they hadn't been given any defensive measures. The uninfected workers of Jack's surrendered convoy would've verified the half-zoms followed Jack's and Jill's verbal commands. Despite that knowledge, she apparently couldn't figure out how to reprogram the soldiers to follow her.

So instead, she had deafened them.

The fighting was dying down, but the violence hadn't. All around, weapons whipped through the air, the thunks, and shlunks, and the sound of wet bloody impacts. The train, station floor, and her people splattered in sick garnet.

CHAPTER SEVENTEEN
THE TRAIN

Audra avoided glancing at the pools of sticky blood and fragments of flesh that decorated the station floor while she directed the people. Bodies sorted and adrenaline fading, energy levels were plummeting. Audra recognized their need to regroup if she was ever going to convince them to board the train.

She encouraged them to wash up, to change from their blood-soaked clothes, and to eat as much as they could handle. Marcos circulated drinking water. Satomi treated the injured. And Ryder organized barricades to keep the train from being recalled. Jack and Peter were nowhere to be found.

After baths and clothing had been distributed, Uno citizens disappeared into their homes, reappearing with coverings and trinkets to dress their deceased. Even in a place where possessions were so few, they surrounded their lost with respect. Survival had been the only focus for so long, but they had returned to keepsakes and giving. They couldn't go back. They had to fight for what they had achieved.

Atop one of the covered bodies sat a small wooden elephant. Audra touched its trunk. While they had to push back toward keepsakes, Belinda had never wandered from them. Her days were spent whittling her animals, leaving them here or there for others to find. Audra didn't allow herself to consider if this was one of hers.

There was work to do.

With all gathered around, Audra reported on the obvious, "Somehow, Lysent got word of our attack. Someone either here or elsewhere — another township maybe — betrayed us."

"How 'bout your boy in Lysent?" asked a man in the crowd.

"Possibly his connection there," Audra conceded. "Lysent sent these half zoms to destroy us. But they didn't. We're still here. Now, we need to make our move before the traitor has a chance to report back."

There were murmurs. Some showed agreement. Most did not. They all sounded tired.

"I know you all fought hard. We will have reinforcements. We just have to pick them up. They'll have our backs. They'll help us."

A few more nods.

"Lysent sent those half zoms to us. They didn't send them evenly throughout the towns. They sent them ALL here. You know why? Because they're scared of you. They're scared of Uno. They know they've treated you wrong and they know you're a threat. Are you?"

"Yes!" came the cries.

"If you're willing to fight more to get what we need, let's gather the weapons, some food for the road, and board this train. You know the horror you felt this morning? Lysent will know that same feeling. They sent half zoms to destroy the thing they fear most — us."

The crowd cheered and readied themselves. And Audra hoped she was doing the right thing.

Within thirty minutes, they were boarding the train. After saying goodbye to loved ones, they settled on stray crates and on the floor, which unfortunately smelled of urine and moist flesh.

Audra and Marcos pulled the barricades off the track and joined the crew in the cab. Ryder pulled on a lever and they began moving forward. She eased them up to speed, sights set on the next township.

They had found Jack and Peter, and they sat in the back of the cab. Audra tried to explain to Peter why his safe word didn't work, but she got no response — just unfocused eyes and periodic I should have never's and so sorry's.

Audra's next objective was to not get sick. She had never moved so fast before. Well, she guessed she had in cars years ago, but she could hardly remember that. It didn't feel like this. Her stomach sloshed. Her head spun. Satomi wretched in the back, which made Audra follow suit.

"Can you slow it down?" asked Audra.

"This is the slowest operating speed. It's an express train, you know," Ryder answered.

If the next township wasn't surprised by the arrival of the blood-streaked train, the outpouring of people doubled over with motion sickness guaranteed their confusion.

"Oh heavens! We knew something was wrong when the train flew by without dropping off any goods and completely off schedule…" one man rambled as he gave hugs, touched arms, and shook as many hands as he could. He called out to others even while he continued. "We sent a scout? Did he arrive? We were going to all come to your rescue if we heard there was trouble. We're so glad you're here. How did you take the train?"

Audra was surprised to hear a small pause where the lithe man was actually expecting an answer. She explained to them in a few short sentences what had happened.

"We need to get going," she said.

"Wait! It's still on?" His blond curls bounced on his head.

"Yes. They won't expect it. They'll assume those half zoms wiped us out and we'll regroup to possibly fight another day. They won't expect us blazing in on this bloody train."

He nodded vigorously and barked commands behind him. "Let's go fellows! The war is still on!"

There was a hustle and bustle as the people began filing out with their weapons.

"Do you have any citizens that disagree with this?" asked Audra. She knew with each township the fighters would become increasingly the minority.

He made a half shrug. "As soon as they saw someone Lysent-cured go mad, they lost the argument. They might not come with us, but they know it's the right thing to do. We all know it's the right thing to do."

Audra nodded and then helped the men pile things into the train.

"No women wanted to come?"

The man suddenly turned reticent. "We're not

sacrificing our women.”

Audra's eyes shrank as she assessed him. She didn't know what to make of him and she really needed him on her side.

“Do any want to come?” She pressed. “Other women from the other townships are coming.” She tried not to point out the obvious.

“That's the other townships' problem,” he said. His eyes flashed with ice. He wasn't going to budge.

Audra really didn't have time for this. She nodded and went into the buildings to help others. While there, she spread the word that anyone who wanted to come was welcome and could sneak onto the train.

With each trip to carry stuff onto the train, she saw new messages painted on the train's silver sides.

Down with Lysent.

Uno Forever.

Stand with us.

In the next township — half of them had no idea what was happening.

“Are you infected? Where are the goods? What happened to the train?” the people asked on high alert.

And only half of those who knew, wanted to come. They hadn't even reached Dunnbreak yet and dissenters were becoming few and unwilling.

“Skip the rest of the towns. If they want to fight, they're not far from Choros,” she told Ryder. Over the intercom, Audra warned her passengers of Dunnbreak's actions and their probable sellout.

“What do you think we'll find at Choros?” asked Ryder.

Audra wished she had the slightest idea.

*   *   *

Ryder approached the train station at Choros, Lysent's home, slowly. Audra had been sure that Lysent had been informed of both the results of the half zom attack and their movement to Choros. How could they not? Their shepherd had stopped reporting back and the bloody train streaked down the rail line.

And yet, the two guards who stood over the perimeter fence made no action against them. And now within their fences, the train sighed to a stop in front of an empty station platform.

Audra decided to immediately let the people out. The rail could be boobytrapped, and even if not, the sooner they got fresh air, the better. The station was a short distance from Choros proper. Past there, Lysent headquarters.

Audra and Peter were the last to leave the cab. He had composed himself since the encounter with his army. With steady breaths and the ability to maintain eye contact, Jack no longer felt it necessary to be at his immediate side and helped others off the train.

Before exiting, Audra opened the top pocket of her backpack. She pulled out a syringe intended for her sister. She had kept it safe for many days and months afterwards, to save someone else. Now, she hoped, being as worthless as it was, that it would actually save them all.

"What is that?" asked Peter as Audra put the antidote in her pocket. "You know those don't work anymore, right?"

Audra giggled at the joke. "It's how we get to Larange."

Peter's eyebrows rose, but he did not pry.

Audra jumped down and signaled for everyone to follow her to the Lysent plaza. Just inside what would be considered the township's line, where the buildings began, sat Dwyn. He rested on the dusty ground with his back and head up against the wall of a building.

"It's about time," he said, jumping up and worried.

"We got delayed. You know how trains are."

"No. I don't," he said, not excited that she was joking at a time like this. They shared a quick hug. He was warm. Too warm. She made no mention of it as he walked with her and all their people.

"Corette? The network? Anyone?" she asked in whispers.

"Yes, some. They are ready when you are. I'll send the signal." Dwyn gave a sharp-keyed whistle. One they used often in the woods.

Audra stopped herself from asking about Corette's motivations and Dwyn's intentions. It really wasn't time for such trivial matters.

"I need a favor from you," she started.

She couldn't let down her people. And they wouldn't understand, but this was how they got Lysent to bow without battle. She had never intended for them to fight. They'd lose a fight, even if they won. They'd lose people and that wasn't acceptable to Audra. She was here to save her people. And that's what they were now. In these final moments, they were her people.

"Anything," he said.

She spoke in a hushed voice. "I need you to bite me."

Dwyn stopped in his tracks and stared at her, deciding if it was one of her jokes. "Hell no," he said, finally understanding.

"Shh! Please. I need to infect Greenly. It's the only way to convince her to work on a cure — when she needs it herself."

Dwyn gave her a hug. "You don't have to do that."

"You don't understand, Dwyn."

"I do," he said. "I'll do it."

"I can't ask you to do that."

"You're not." He reached for her hand. She let him take it and he put it against his face and neck to let her in on his feverish secret, which she already knew. She felt tears prickle in the corners of her eyes.

You don't have to do it alone.

That's what he had told her. That's what she had told Manny. Now it was time to accept it, even if it meant risking Dwyn's life instead of her own.

They walked in silence for a few moments. Peter coughed behind them and drew up closer.

"Hey, I want to talk to Greenly," he requested. "Maybe she'll cave when she finds out she isn't the only surviving manager. Maybe we can pull corporate on her."

Peter had seemed so broken up over what he had done. Audra wasn't sure how stable he was now. She barely knew the man. "She rattled their eardrums. It's not your fault. We don't blame you."

"Oh, but you should. I created them. That's why they are out in this world. I didn't see hope, so I made things worse. But you continue to strive toward a cure. You've always made sure people are treated as people."

"Not always," Audra's voice broke. "But I try now."

"Me too," Peter replied.

As they reached the township, many people

watched through windows. Some opened doors and stood outside to watch the small mass of people with weapons quietly march toward Lysent. No one had ever seen so many people convene in the township, not even for major announcements. There were lots of murmurs and discussions, but at least no one was pulling weapons on them. They were more curious than anything else of the people who lived in townships they'd never visited.

"Why are you here?" asked a man, standing on a business stoop.

"We're requesting Greenly work on a cure," stated Audra.

"There IS a cure," the man scoffed. "Why don't you just play by the rules?"

"We didn't mess up the cure. People everywhere are regressing. Lysent needs to stop telling you lies and start trying to help for once."

Some joined their ranks as they continued down the main drag. Many others followed just to see what would happen. And several more tucked away, fearing the outcome of a meeting between an overbearing government and ungrateful constituents. The adults told their children to stay home as they promised to be back. Just another boring announcement, they told them.

CHAPTER EIGHTEEN
AN AUDIENCE

They marched down the main road to the wrought iron fencing surrounding Lysent Corporation proper. Lysent Corporation was a campus of buildings, which to Audra's knowledge, had not closed a single day during the pandemic. When things went to shit, Lysent just kept its employees inside. Over the next several years, the township of Choros developed at Lysent's front door to serve as a public market and to house a farming community.

Larange Greenly seemed to be expecting them. The tall decorative gate had been swung completely open and no one stood at its perimeter to modulate the flow of guests. An open gate, an invitation. Lysent had not confronted them at the station, because it wanted to confront them here.

Audra led over a hundred people into the plaza. Directly across, past the cherub-covered fountain, sat Lysent's primary building, often called headquarters. The pristine, unbroken windows towered on the face of the white mansion. Pillars and a long veranda graced the facade. The front often served as a stage for Greenly. Even now it had a podium placed in its center.

Before they even had a chance to settle and wonder what to do next, the massive doors opened to a petite woman. The woman could never resist an opportunity to tell her constituents they were ungrateful. Large bulky guards moved in front of her as they exited onto the veranda. They moved to either side when Greenly settled behind the podium.

Audra could not imagine a tighter bun of hair. It not only flattened crow's feet, but went as far as changing the shape of her eyes. The salt and pepper was more salt than Audra remembered. Was it age or the stress incurred by building an empire around an ineffective cure? Otherwise she looked well-rested. She had probably slept well knowing she was sending a disposable army into the heart of the rebellion.

She wouldn't sleep well tonight.

Larange Greenly looked directly at Audra and spoke to her from her perch. "Did I not tell you that you were not allowed in this place?"

"I don't remember. Did you?" she couldn't help but answer. Ryder gave her an elbow. This apparently wasn't the time.

"I see you brought friends," she waved her hand dismissively over her community, people she should know as fellow survivalists.

"Yes. You'll see that your towns all want the same thing. To be safe."

"And how is stampeding into my corporation safe?" she asked a little too fast. Audra knew her temper was already simmering at the surface.

"It's not the safety of your corporation we're

worried about," she explained.

"May a few of us could come up there? It is difficult to yell."

The guards, who Audra didn't think could tense up any more, did.

"And why would you come up here?" she asked. "Do you want to kill me?" she laughed.

Audra did want to kill her, but she thought it better not to speak the truth on that one. For now, she'd settle for a conversation and possibly a conversion.

"I want to discuss this, leaders to leader. I don't want there to be a disagreement. We just came to show you how serious we were. We are."

"You do not want to fight?"

"No."

"That is very smart of you. Yes, you may come up and negotiate your surrender."

"We want to fight," Ryder whispered hoarsely. "We are willing to fight."

"I know, but maybe we don't have to fight."

Audra stepped toward the stage. Peter and Dwyn joined her.

"Please remove all weapons. They are not allowed on the stage," a guard barked.

Audra raised her hands in a surrender motion. "Of course, of course." She gingerly and slowly pulled weapons off her, being clear with her actions. Dwyn and Peter did the same.

Afterwards, Peter cleared his throat. "I know you have the original virus, Larange. All the corporate branches received virus and antivirals for distribution." His tone was professional.

"Who are you?" she asked.

"I'm a Lysent scientist from the Washington, DC

branch."

There were murmurs in the crowd, both in her group and those watching. Peter gave them credibility. Suddenly there was another corporate voice outside of Larange Greenly and her direct employees.

Greenly kept her cool. "We distribute the antiviral in a sustainable way. You don't have a say without knowing our economic system."

"You're providing an antiviral for the original virus, but it's not effective for the current virus rampaging through your region. We request that you give up the original virus samples you have, so real work can be done to help the people. Otherwise, you're taking advantage here, selling snake oil for food."

Voices began to rise from the crowd, even from behind the fence. Audra hid a smile. The townships loved authority, and Peter was displaying a lot of it — at Greenly's expense. Even if you didn't care — especially if you didn't care — about the antiviral, you didn't want to trade your food for it. The basis of Greenly's empire was crumbling to a hungry winter and a down-talking official.

Pink splotched Greenly's papery skin. Her left eye twitched.

"Get off my stage!" she screamed, rushing toward Peter, waving her hand as if to shoo him away.

As Greenly closed the distance, Dwyn leaped in a forward tackle. He almost made it, but a large fist came up by Greenly's ear and met Dwyn's face. A hollow crunch and Dwyn's task was left incomplete. And yet, Greenly's screech, shrill and panicked, still filled the stage.

Arms, legs, and fists flew.

A guard pulled Peter off Greenly, not the other way

around. A small spray of blood. Twice as large as Peter, the guard plowed his heavy fist into the elderly man. Peter fell back and didn't move. Audra tried to enter the fray. The same strong arm struck her gut. Lower ribs stung as her small body was thrown off the veranda onto the concrete below.

Blood.

Blood had flown before Peter's jaw broke. Audra didn't understand.

The guards pulled back revealing Larange, who sat awkwardly on the ground in her black pencil skirt. Her hand covered her left cheek. Crimson blood flowed, a stark contrast to her pale skin — which paled further.

Still holding her cheek, she screamed, "Search him!"

One of the men began ripping clothes off the unconscious body. He held up a thin arm, its flesh shredded. A grievous injury.

Peter hadn't flinched when they patted him down. Audra hadn't even recognized when it happened. He had gotten up in his soldier's face. He had done it on purpose.

"Kill him! Kill them all!" Greenly raged.

Jack rushed the stage, followed quickly by Audra. Larange backed away, but Jack moved to his father's body. He held him close to his chest and tried to wake him. Greenly's face went from pale to fuchsia. She jumped on the guard, physically trying to pull him into action. He brushed her off like someone would a small child.

"Kill them now!" she yelled again. The guards traded glances before continuing their stillness.

Frustrated, she turned to go inside, but the doors swung open before she reached them. She stepped back in surprise as thirty employees filed out.

"What is this?!" she called out. Steam could have risen from her diamond-studded ears.

"We all want the same thing. Safety. From the virus. You created," said a Ukrainian woman Audra assumed to be Corette.

Audra noticed Clyde and Rosie among those standing on the veranda. Clyde's thick sun-worn skin in soft white robes. Rosie's black ringlets shook in anger. The crowd was angry too.

Shouts for Greenly to be killed.

"We all just want the same thing — all of us," said Audra. She pulled the syringe from her pocket. "You can take it, and you'll be safe for a while. Then, we can all work together to make it permanent."

Greenly turned pale again before her eyes darkened and she spat at Audra. Muscles glistened from her cheek.

"You ungrateful bastards!" she shouted into the crowd. "I used that make-shift cure to build this place — a safe place! None of you deserve to be cured. YOU CAN ALL ROT!"

She then stood up straight and smoothed out her suit. She cleared her throat. "I'm sorry you haven't been able to see what I've provided here," she said as she reached into her pocket and pulled out a device.

Audra and Dwyn rushed her at the same time, but Greenly's hand had already pressed and released. A smile tore through her face.

*　　*　　*

How they hadn't noticed the smell, she wasn't sure. Maybe the lingering scent of the half zoms and the train had disguised the smell of the herd. The wind was just right. Or, they were just all distracted by the woman on the stage.

The gate rattled and twisted with the pressing force of bodies funneling into the plaza. Fresh and long decayed alike. A thousand at least. The shock almost moved Audra's stomach to upend itself.

This was the purpose of the corrals.

The corrals were never to keep the townships safe. They were never to cure when life improved.

They were Greenly's contingency plan.

Plaza exits blocked with zoms pouring in, Greenly rushed inside the mansion. Audra fought the urge to give chase. It wasn't just her now.

"Follow her! Get inside!" Audra yelled to the crowd unnecessarily as they pressed into the narrow entrance. She jumped down and helped people over the stage. Arms and legs and panicked panting.

As the stage filled with bodies, Audra fought the flood to place herself between the people and the zoms. She pulled on the arm of a woman on the ground.

"No!" the woman screamed out. "This is our punishment. We know these people. We know them. And now they'll know us!" she babbled.

Audra let go of the woman's arm violently. She didn't have time for such nonsense. Her words were words Audra had repeated so often. Those healthy were not exceptional in any way except for their obligation to help those in need. But they turned their backs on them — and now their backs were probably going to be consumed.

She had never seen such a herd. Their skin dripped from their facial bones. Flesh barely clung to arms and legs. Torsos pulled apart. There was nothing to them and yet they were still moving, jagged infectious bones, claws, and teeth. Some bodies seemed to have merged, pressed together by the mob, masses moving like a rushing current.

"Do not engage! Go!" she yelled even as she sank her recovered knife into an empty eye socket. The body fell off Audra's knife and onto the ground. There were hundreds more. One down in a sea of a thousand.

"Don't close the doors!" someone cried. The edges of the tall doors wavered into sight as people pressed against others entering.

Audra swore under her breath. They'd all be able to escape inside if they could pull themselves together. Even staring into the depths of ripped flesh and jutting bone, she almost preferred its company to those she was protecting. She moved with the crowds as the final retreating and protective line. A bag of flesh staggered to Audra. With a swift kick from her boot, its entire skull gave way like a deflated ball. It fell to the ground and did not get back up.

Two down.

Lysent hadn't even managed to maintain their zombie hordes. Exposure had left them soft and dying. Their bone spongy. But to these people who had been sheltered, it was a horror, stuff of old nightmares that clung to their brains in the darkest of nights.

The zoms surged over and around the stage. The podium fell and disappeared. The zoms close to her tripped on the steps, but she couldn't risk any more kill strikes. She'd get overwhelmed.

Audra jumped onto the veranda, through the zoms, and sprinted as the last living person outside. The doors nipped at her heels, sending her flying into the marble lobby. Hallways branched off on the first floor but Audra knew all exits only led to the now-buried plaza. Marcos and Dwyn ran by, pushing Rosie's solid mahogany desk, slamming it against the front door. Rosie stood where her desk had been with an armful of papers and a stapler. She added them to the pile atop the filing cabinet, but it was quickly whisked away as well, sending papers flying.

"I never…" she muttered. Her eyes bulged as she stood alone in the chaos.

Audra escorted the woman to the stairs, placing her paper-worn fingers onto the railing. Rosie followed the stream of people seeking higher ground. Along the edge of the stairs, a steady flow of melee weapons passed hands.

Audra slipped her wrist into the leather braid of a sharpened machete. It was a weapon too large for her, almost unwieldy, but favorable in this choke point situation. Ryder sheathed a hunting blade, attaching the belt to her waist. She held a clawed hammer in her hand.

Even though they were hidden from sight, the tide's trajectory could not be changed. Bone, flesh, and death smashed against the walls and windows with increasing velocity and increasing height as bodies piled upon the building. The glass heaved and let out high-pitched complaints with the pressure. The door bulged with the heaviness. The furniture jolted.

Audra directed all those with weapons to stand adjacent to the future entryways. She didn't have to count heads to know that the majority of her defense line was composed of Osprey Point, not Uno and most surely not Choros.

The ever-illuminated lobby went dim as the windows filled. With pops and hisses, the glass shattered. Pressure, not individual exertion brought the zombies forth. As they passed through, jagged window pieces created tangled threads of flesh. Audra brought her machete down like a guillotine parallel to the window's frame, slicing off portions of emerging faces.

The clots and clogs of zombies multiplied and bulged. The cracking of glass, wood splintering, and the groan of office furniture signaled the impending swell. Audra pulled her group. They retreated to the next floor as the sick crept in like unwanted water.

CHAPTER NINETEEN
CHASING EXTINCTION

Audra had never been on the higher floors of Lysent headquarters. A large parlor met her at the landing. A mahogany desk, identical to the one in the lobby, stood adjacent to a double door with elaborate carvings. Larange Greenly's office, no doubt. Audra weaved her way through the trembling men who hadn't helped defend the first floor, and she slipped in to see if the CEO was in.

The rectangular office faced the plaza, filling the office with beautiful natural light that made this building a favorite of Lysent. Audra wondered if the second-story windows would also be eventually carpeted by the dead. The wall to her right had inset shelves lined with books. Old tomes of business law, calligraphic fiction titles, and everything in between, stocked to the high ceiling. Opposite, a three-dimensional map of the world hung on the wall. Thin metallic continents seemingly floated on their ocean-blue canvas. Gold pin heads scattered on the map, locations of Lysent branches, Audra assumed.

And in the center of her windowed wall, the manager of this particular branch paid her no mind. Small shoulders over straight posture, she had remade her silvery bun. The hair swirled into itself like a nautilus. She stood at the window, overseeing her advancing infected troops as they attacked her keep.

"Did you want to go down with the ship?" Audra asked her coolly.

"You brought down this ship," she said without turning.

Osprey Point and the townships had requested medical care, else a change in government. In turn, Greenly had unleashed hundreds of zombies to wipe out the population. How the latter wasn't to blame for the sinking ship was beyond Audra's understanding and she assumed, beyond even Greenly's capacity for explanation.

"You have shepherds out there," Audra said.

No answer from Greenly.

"They could lead these zoms out. You've made your point. You're willing to see this whole place destroyed before you give up power, but is that what you really want? Do you want to die here?"

Greenly turned, wine red blossoming along the tissues of her wound.

"Yes, if it means I get to watch all of you die first. You've brought this on yourselves and me. You're right. The cure is no more. You've sentenced me to death, and I'm carrying out that sentence."

Audra maneuvered around the marble-capped desk.

"It doesn't have to be a death sentence. You could clear this place out and we can go back to normal business, studying and working toward a cure."

"For whom? Like you'd give it to me." A muscle in her cheek twitched.

"You think I'm like you?" asked Audra, disgusted. "Picking. Choosing. Selling cures? I would gladly provide you with any available treatment. It would give you time to be tried for your crimes against your people."

Greenly digested Audra's proposal.

"I have the upper hand," Greenly replied. "I have the zombies."

In Audra's hand, she had a dagger.

The zombies below couldn't prevent Audra from digging a claw deep into Greenly's bun, pulling to expose her wrinkled neck, and bleeding her out. Greenly didn't have the zoms. The zoms had them. Soon, all of them, in hungry, horrible ways.

Greenly continued despite the nearby blade, "I had high expectations for you — fiery and angry — a great combination, one I'm intimately familiar with. But you're weak," she spat. "You've always been weak. First it was your sister. You dragged around that corpse baggage for years. And now it's these people. Like me, you don't need them."

Greenly thought Audra's connections made her weak. By wiping out the masses, the ones left standing would be stronger. But what would really be left? Dwyn believed no one should go about this life alone. Audra considered the place she stood, on a precipice overlooking an undulating sea of the dead. She'd never want to be the last. And she didn't have to be.

Like me.

For someone facing death, Greenly was disturbingly calm. Her palms and collar dry. Her breathing deep and rhythmic. Audra followed

Greenly's eyes. She no longer looked at the masses of gray rot surging below them. She looked beyond them. Just beyond Choros.

It was quiet there.

Audra began kicking around the room, snooping for Greenly's escape. The bookcases, although promising based on memories of weekend morning cartoons, did not demonstrate any secretive features. No trap door underneath her desk. Audra pulled the map sculpture off the wall. Behind it, a stepping stool and safety harness sat in a hidden shaft. The shaft's built-in ladder led up, Audra assumed to the roof.

"When were you going to go?" asked Audra.

"I was going to sneak away when things got chaotic. I still might, darling. Looks like they're coming up the stairs…"

"Chaos, huh?" Audra confiscated the safety harness then swung the office doors open. "She's in here," Audra called.

As Greenly was dragged into the parlor, Audra checked on the status of the first floor. The first floor could no longer be seen. Zombies ebbed and flowed on the stairs, working their way up then being pulled back down by their own. The sounds and scents would eventually draw them up like the tide.

The townships had always traded freedom for protection. Now it was time to stand on their own. Audra directed them to protect the second floor where they currently resided. After grabbing a coil of rope from the armory, she called Ryder and Dwyn into Greenly's office. Satomi followed tightly on their heels. The safety harness and Greenly's speech of solo endeavors hinted that her escape was not one for the masses. But if the zombies could be redirected, they all might survive another day.

Audra climbed up the ladder first, the safety harness slung on her shoulder. She pulled on the latch at the top and light streamed through. Climbing onto the flat roof, Dwyn followed right behind her.

"Come on up," she directed down the shaft. She heard Satomi and Ryder share a kiss before one of the women started up the ladder.

At first Audra only saw electrical cables. If Greenly was going to use them to escape, it would have been an escape of a different kind. One came from the lines that ran along the town. And there was another that reached to a lower building, as a secondary supply. No one had bothered to wire the building up to the main supply? Why not? But no, they had. The one that actually held power to deliver to the building was partially hidden from view by trees.

As Audra approached it, she realized it was only disguised as electrical. It was no such thing, but just a line anchored from building to building.

Audra walked to the edge of the roof. She looked down at the expanse of zoms that filled the plaza. It was like a slow-moving and foul-smelling fire that had them retreating to higher ground.

"Oh my," whispered Ryder.

Audra stepped into the harness and began to pull it up when clanking steps sounded in the passageway.

Larange Greenly's mussed gray hair came into view. She raised one of her hands in surrender as she continued her way up. Her face had drained of color except the crusting darkness that lined it.

Audra was impressed with her gall and surprised she had escaped the others. They must have been more worried about their survival than about the malefactor.

Audra felt the same. She pulled out her knife.

"What are you doing up here?" Audra asked.

"I'm here to bargain. You can have the original virus in return for allowing me over that line."

Audra stepped out of the harness. Greenly moved to accept it and Audra kicked it to the side.

"We're going to get the original virus anyway. You're done," said Audra.

"But you're done too." Greenly tilted her head at an almost maniacal angle, even more disturbing with the rip in her cheek.

Audra blinked in disbelief. Greenly was willing to sacrifice this entire corner of the world, just to say I told you so. There was no helping this woman. And without help, she wouldn't be able to escape the roof. Because no matter what Greenly thought, she couldn't do it alone.

Audra pivoted to pick up the harness. Small feet pitter pattered behind her on the gravel. Audra spun around in time to receive the small woman. Greenly hadn't turned, but she might as well have. She snarled and snapped. Spittle fell on Audra's face.

Audra grabbed the woman's shoulders. They felt thin and decrepit. Muscles separated from bone. Larange really wasn't that powerful after all. Audra threw the woman off her. She skittered on the gravel, her feet off the building's edge.

Audra walked over to the woman who had watched the world fall then kicked it again. Larange had so many choices. She could have celebrated the fences, instead of bartering them. What if Audra had pulled her sister into town and Greenly had provided treatment? What if she had worked on a cure from the beginning, instead of doling out false hope to get ahead? Maybe, they would have survived.

Greenly scrambled to stand, but struggled to do so. Mouths below undulated in the background.

"You've killed us all," admitted Audra to the woman in black.

A cracked sneer broke on Larange's face. "Good," she giggled.

Audra's boot smashed into Greenly's spotted face. With a hard push, she slipped farther off the roof. She didn't call out for help that wasn't coming. Greenly's fingers dug deep into the gravel for a moment before straightening, the woman's arms and torn face falling from sight.

The feeding frenzy roared like a wave.

*　　*　　*

Without a word to the others, Audra returned to the safety harness and stepped inside it.

It wasn't her fault Greenly had refused to call it quits.

Satomi's hands shook as she latched the buckles, and pulled the straps tight. Having last been tested on Greenly, the straps didn't require much adjustment from one small figure to another. Audra tied the rope to the harness so it could be retrieved for Dwyn's use. She then used the harness's accoutrements to attach herself to the anchored cable.

She got close to the edge. The sea of zoms, the smell, the heights. Audra pulled in a deep breath and swallowed the bile that threatened to make itself known. Pulling herself onto the cable, she crossed her legs over. She moved her arms in the back and forth motion to carry her across, focused on the crisp blue above.

The cable sagged with her weight, but it had to be fine, right? She pretended there were no zoms below her. She pretended that she was floating through the sky. She was going down and down and the cable felt like it was falling unnecessarily low. The roaring got louder as she caught the attention of zoms.

She knew they were clawing at the air and at each other, trying to reach her. Their muscles straining tight and snapping against bones. All it would take would be a zombie with some hops, and she'd be torn from her hook. Bitten and chewed, her insides sprawling on the ground. And, as Audra remembered from so many times in her childhood, it would take forever — absolutely forever — for the person to die. She'd watch her body being parceled out before death caught up.

"You're there, Audra!" yelled out Dwyn. "Feel around with your feet!"

It went against her instinct to take her feet off the cable. She lowered them slowly, so slowly, until she felt something solid. Pea gravel. The roof. She dug her heels in and pulled her body farther onto the roof. She didn't feel safe until she had ass on gravel.

She unbuckled her harness and let Ryder pull it back along its route. Soon Dwyn was hooked up and began his descent. The cable sagged even more with Dwyn's weight, the heavier of the two, and Audra almost cried for him to stop and turn around, he was so close. The zoms snatched at the air right below his back. They could almost grab him. But Audra knew she had gotten through, and it probably looked scary as well. Ryder didn't seem to have any fears, so Audra stayed quiet, but murmured small prayers to no one.

With Dwyn's ass safe on the gravel, Audra jumped onto his body, pressing into a deep kiss.

"It's not because I almost died just now, is it?" he laughed, nervously.

"No, it's because you don't make me weaker. You make me stronger."

Audra finally knew her reason. Home didn't have to be a place to run from.

"You in?" she asked.

"Until the cows come home," he assured her.

Audra glanced down at the mob.

"And after," he added.

On the single-story building, the zombies pulled even closer. They reached to them. Their eyes wide and their mouths gaping. They were rotting inside and out. They would soon be gone from this world, but not soon enough. Audra picked her favorite non-zombie side of the building. She lowered herself down, and then gently dropped the rest of the way.

Dwyn followed.

"Grab my pack from the train," Audra directed Dwyn as they landed in Chorus.

"Where will you be?"

"In the market," she yelled over her shoulder as she raced away.

Audra found her destination deserted save a couple of zoms distracted by the same reason she had come. Bags of bones and skin reached into the hog sty. One had fallen in and was slowly shambling around the pen. The animals rested until it got close, then ran off. Run. Rest. Run.

Audra jumped in, dodging both the zom inside the pen and the mouths and arms hanging onto the perimeter. She rushed and dove, trying to grab a hog — hopefully a small one she could carry. She thought of all the zoms swarming and how everyone was going to perish as she ran around chasing pigs. She lunged again, and this time caught the small one. Dwyn had returned with her pack. He jumped in and helped her tie the hog up with the rope from her bag. Knots she had taught him.

Toting the pig, they marched back to the plaza, positioned themselves at the gate. The masses had their backs to them. She pulled two noisemakers from her bag.

Audra dragged her knife through the pig's body. The pig squealed an awful sound. Organs slipped. Drenched in hot blood, she turned on her noisemaker, sirens blaring. Dwyn did the same. They stood there, waiting, steeled to stay as long as they could to collect as many as possible.

Heads turned, bodies followed. It seemed to only be a small movement at first. As the first approached, Audra and Dwyn took a few steps back, dragging the screaming animal by the rope. They stared down the horde with its slowly turning tide. Audra saw Dwyn shiver. She put a hand on his arm, leaving a smear of blood.

"Oops," she said.

Dwyn shook his head and smiled before they began their backward jog. Just moments later, they had to turn and sprint. Their following had become less of a crowd and more like an avalanche, threatening to swallow them whole. The narrow drag created a funnel pushing zombie atop zombie and still climbing. They were fast. They were falling. They kept moving.

"You got this group?" she asked.

Dwyn's eyes widened as he realized why she was asking.

She pulled the pig rope out of his hands and threw it on the ground, abandoning their bait. Now Dwyn could run faster. And Audra peeled off.

They hadn't pulled off the loop-de-loop maneuver in so long and never with this many zoms, but it also kind of felt like home. Knowing they were partners, she finally allowed him the first wave. She no longer had to do everything herself.

Audra let the dreaded crowd pass as she cut back behind other buildings. She approached the plaza once more. All the zoms that were leaving had left. Those inside were left inside, not getting enough stimulus from the plaza to find their way out.

A smear on the ground indicated what remained of Greenly. Physically, she was gone, but the damage of her reign remained. Audra had imagined killing Greenly often and in so many ways. But now, she only felt a burden on her heart for all the work left to be done. Greenly had dealt them a hand they might not be able to survive.

Crunching sounds above told Audra she wasn't alone. All her people stood atop Lysent's headquarters, safe from the zombies inside.

"You all OK?" she asked.

Ryder replied. "Yes, no problem here. Take your time."

Audra tied her last noisemaker to her bag before stepping deep into the plaza, toward the building's now-many openings. Picking up an abandoned piece of lumber, she broke all the glass left in the Lysent windows.

Space and noise.

She couldn't do anything about the desk and filing cabinet that partially blocked the door, but they had found their way in, they could find their way out.

Audra returned to the center of the plaza, not far from the bloody intersection of concrete and remains. She turned on the noisemaker and lit her flare. Sound rang from one ear to the other. Chemical smoke touched her lungs. And the fleshy undead wandered toward her. Her head spun. How long had she been fighting today?

Somehow she realized it would be dark soon.

Audra put her hands on her knees and let herself be sick. She was so tired. She waited the last possible moments, covered in the blood of the undead, of swine, of enemies. Layered in her own vomit and tears. Now, she'd just have to run. After all the hard work, she just had to run.

Or you know, get eaten.

Audra turned, but someone snagged her bag. Faces flashed in her mind. A haggard Greenly rising up, forcing her to take notice. A gaunt Belinda, willing her to see. Audra jerked away and freed herself. She couldn't play to the visions invading her mind. Even if they were so inviting. It was appropriate that the many faces of the lost would run her from town. She hadn't been able to save them.

What would be left in the wake of these zombies? Would they survive, find a cure? Or were they slowly dying like their brethren, corralled by their mistakes?

Audra sprinted out onto the road as the sun was setting. She wouldn't have to answer these questions alone.

And that was a start.

EPILOGUE

It took Audra many weeks to find her small pop-up tent out in the woods. She breathed a small prayer before calling out. Thankfully, it was answered.

A large organized group had pulled apart the community at the grocery store, taking all their food and fuel. From the description, Audra wondered if it was Lysent goons. Everyone had scattered to find their way. Haleigh and Eliza were on the run once again.

But Audra had made a promise.

"Thank you," said Haleigh for the hundredth time.

Audra acknowledged her and handed Eliza a piece of jerky to walk with. She felt it necessary to warn Haleigh again. "You understand we've made good progress, but it's not done. It might take some time."

Haleigh giggled. "You understand that we thought he was gone? Gone for years. We're happy to see him in any state, in any part. If you cure him, wow… fantastic. If you don't, we'll still have seen him, been with him. We'll no longer be alone."

Audra did understand.

They stopped frequently for blisters and snacks. Audra carried Eliza when she tired. And they camped just off the road for the night. While she tempered Haleigh's expectations, she had full confidence in her scientists. With the original virus retrieved from Lysent's labs, they had quickly found mutations that needed to be addressed. They were going to get a cure.

Gordon would be cured.

Dwyn.

Lisa.

Late in the next day, Audra paused.

"We have to get off the road now, and go through the woods," she said to the pair.

"Is that OK, Eliza?" Audra knelt down to ask.

Eliza shook her head. Her eyes wide. "I'm scared. The woods are scary."

Audra looked into the woods and while she usually saw glittering light, obstacles to dodge, and a chance to move freely, now she saw what Eliza saw. It was dark, gloomy, scratchy, and full of unknowns.

It was what Belinda saw.

"It is scary, but sometimes you have to do scary things. Sometimes they end up not being scary. Sometimes they are. But if you don't move forward, you'll never know."

"Will you be there with me?"

"I will."

"And mom?"

"Until the cows come home." Eliza gave her a confused look. "Yes, she will," Audra clarified.

"That's enough then. We can do it together."

Accepting support while moving forward. Audra

couldn't force, but she could help.

Eliza took Audra's hand as they stepped into the woods.

NOTE FROM THE AUTHOR

Thank you for following Audra and me through the Georgian woods and the zombie apocalypse.

Chasing a Cure started as an idea for National Novel Writing Month and grew into a trilogy with gentle feedback and harsh kicks in the butt from my family, writing group, beta readers, and editor. I can't thank them enough.

While the suicides in this trilogy are fictional, suicide is a very real and tragic part of our lives. Please know if you need help there are people waiting to talk to you. You can reach free and confidential emotional support by calling 1-800-273-TALK (8255) or texting HOME to 741-741 in the US or calling 116 123 in the UK.

Follow me on Patreon.conm/rmhamrick for weekly updates, draft snippets, ebooks and paperbacks.